THE BLUE SANTO MURDER MYSTERY

MARGARET ARMSTRONG

LOST CRIME CLASSICS

www.lostcrimeclassics.com

PEPIK BOOKS

This edition published 2015 by Pepik Books, Blake House, 18 Blake Street, York, YO1 8QH

Copyright © 2015 Pepik Books

The Blue Santo Murder Mystery by Margaret Armstrong (1867-1944) was first published in 1941.

Published by Pepik Books (www.pepikbooks.com) as part of the *Lost Crime Classics* collection.

www.lostcrimeclassics.com

All rights reserved. This book is sold subject to the condition that it shall not, by way of trade or otherwise, be reproduced, lent, re-sold, hired out or otherwise circulated in any form of binding or cover other than that in which it is published and without a similar condition being imposed on the subsequent purchaser.

ISBN: 978-0-9932357-6-4
Printed and bound in the EU

THE BLUE SANTO MURDER MYSTERY

MARGARET ARMSTRONG

LOST CRIME CLASSICS
www.lostcrimeclassics.com

1

Mr Jonathan Carboy, of Carboy and Patterson, 60 Wall Street, stepped briskly out of the train as it came to a stop in the Pennsylvania Terminal, nodded to the nearest porter, indicated one bag among the pile on the platform, and walking rapidly on through various lofty corridors, emerged at length in the waiting room of the Long Island Railroad. As he reached the news-stand he paused.

"Evening papers not in yet?" he demanded.

"Not yet, sir," the porter answered. "Where to, sir?"

"Oyster Bay."

"Twenty-five minutes to wait."

"I'll sit down over there."

He moved to a vacant seat, two trains having just left, the station fly trap, shaken empty, was not yet full again, tipped the porter, sat down, and became immersed in thought.

For the past few days Mr Carboy had been too busy to think. This was the first moment he could call his own. His mind turned at once to a letter that had been handed to him by his partner as he was leaving the office, with the sardonic comment: "Something for you to chew on, old man, while you're gone."

Mr Carboy extracted the letter from an inner pocket, noted that it was from his most profitable client, Mrs Kearny-Pine, at present in Tecos, New Mexico. Ran his eye hastily down the first two pages: "Magnificent scenery. Picturesque pueblo. High altitude. No palpitations as yet. Death of my maid exceedingly inconvenient..." and reached the final paragraph.

"I have decided," it ran, "to change my will. The fortune accumulated by the sagacity of my dear father, which has increased under my stewardship, must be safeguarded, and I shall take steps to prevent its being dissipated by reckless extravagance. But I cannot go into the matter in detail at present as it is time for my constitutional. I will write to you again tomorrow. Trusting that Mrs Carboy and my godchild, little Louisa, are in good health, I remain, Sincerely yours, Louisa Kearny-Pine."

Mr Carboy folded the letter, more than a week old now, and pocketed it with an impatient sigh. Who was to be prevented from squandering the fortune that 'my dear father's' Golden Chain stores had piled up and his daughter had increased? Was it her nephew Algernon? Algy's extravagance was an old old story. Was it her cousin, little Rosalie Colbrook? Rosalie was a nice girl and not at all extravagant.

Or was it her husband she was worrying about? And if so, why? Had the gossip titillating Long Island for the past few weeks come to Mrs Kearny-Pine's ears at last? Did she know that Stephen was having an affair with Mrs Larkin? The beautiful Mrs Larkin, as respectable as she was beautiful, and, therefore, dangerous? Good God, was there no limit to Stephen's folly! Why couldn't a man lucky enough to have married the richest woman in America, the last income tax returns gave his wife that title, satisfy himself with some less conspicuous amour? The latest rumour actually hinted at divorce.

Mr Carboy pocketed the letter with a sigh of annoyance, and glanced about him. Two clerical figures whom he recognized – the Bishop of Manhattan and his chaplain, Mr Cope – were descending the stairs, followed by a luggage-bearing porter. But Mr Carboy felt no desire for conversation; he closed his eyes, affecting deep slumber, hoping to remain unobserved for another ten minutes.

He succeeded. The Bishop and his escort moved sedately onward across the dusty floor and joined the throng already gathering at the Oyster Bay gate.

"No vacant seats, of course," Mr Cope remarked, and added, with some bitterness: "I never enter the Long Island station, sir, without being reminded of Milton's lines: 'They also serve who only *stand* and *wait*' should be inscribed over the entrance."

"To remind us that patience is a virtue?" the Bishop smiled. "Any news of our black sheep? Or rather, our wolf in sheep's clothing?"

"News, but not encouraging, Sir Hubert Pierce called me up this morning. It seems the police traced Weedon to Chicago and lost him! But it's an interesting story. I asked Hubert to take our train, he commutes from Far Rockaway, so that he could report to you in person. There he is now."

A slim, well-dressed young man had emerged from the entrance to the subway and paused to survey the crowd. Mr Cope beckoned. He joined them at the gate and was greeted with affability by the Bishop, who had known the young man since boyhood and was eagerly awaiting his report of the activities of a notorious crook who had recently ventured into the clerical field and was making hay with alarming success.

"Cope tells me that the police lost Weedon in Chicago!" the Bishop exclaimed. "How did that happen?"

"The hare outran the tortoise, sir, as he usually does in real life," Pierce answered. "Weedon was quick and the police were slow. But it might have been worse. Weedon didn't do much business in Chicago. The police missed him by five minutes."

"Have the police any clues?"

"A man answering to his description bought a ticket for San Francisco that same afternoon. They'll get him very shortly now."

Mr Carboy's ten minutes were almost up now. He roused, beckoned to a porter, and affecting to catch sight of his clerical friends with surprise, he hurried to join them.

Greetings were exchanged; Hubert Pierce was introduced. Carboy glanced at the young man with curiosity as they shook hands; he knew this 'gentleman detective' by reputation. It developed that the Bishop was on his way to Oyster Bay for Confirmation.

"Where are you stopping, sir?" Carboy inquired. "Not with Mrs Kearny-Pine, as you usually do, for she is away."

"The rector of Saint Ampelopsis-by-the-Sea is putting me up. Speaking of Mrs Kearny-Pine, you know, of course, that she is now touring the West?"

"Yes. She is in New Mexico at present."

"New Mexico? I should doubt whether so lofty an altitude were altogether salutary for a person with a cardiac affection."

"She seems to be all right. I had a letter from her a few days ago, a business letter. She said the altitude was causing no inconvenience."

"I understand that the campaign designed to ruin her rival, the Peerless Chain, originated with her," Hubert Pierce remarked.

"It did," Carboy nodded. "What's more, she has achieved what she set out to do. It's no secret. All the world will know tomorrow. Peerless is down and out."

"Peerless ruined!" the Bishop exclaimed. "Most gratifying to Mrs Kearny-Pine, no doubt. But less so for Peerless stockholders."

"Well, you can't please everybody."

"This is true," the Bishop admitted. "But the affair will bring her a good deal of adverse criticism, I fear. She may have gone to New Mexico to avoid reporters as well as to enjoy the beauties of nature. Is her husband with her, Hubert?"

"No, indeed Stephen declined with thanks. Stephen had other fish to fry. I suppose you've heard about Stephen and..."

He broke off abruptly, and turned. Someone at the back of the station had let out an exclamation of surprise. It was followed by a confusion of excited questions and still more excited answers, and the rustle of a dozen newspapers all unfolding at once.

"The evening papers!" Mr Carboy exclaimed. "Something startling must have happened."

Mr Carboy stared at the news-stand. The Bishop and Mr Cope stared. Hubert Pierce did not wait to stare. He was already on his way to the news-stand where a boy was handing out papers with the precision of a machine.

"What are they saying, Mr Carboy?" the Bishop demanded. "What is the cause of this commotion?"

Mr Carboy shook his head, and began elbowing a path for the Bishop through the crowd. But Hubert Pierce was already returning.

He slipped an Evening Sun into the Bishop's hand. Across the page a string of huge black letters asked the world:

WHERE IS MRS KEARNY-PINE?

The Bishop groaned. Mr Carboy shuddered. Mr Cope expressed his horror. Hubert Pierce stood silent; bending over the Bishop's shoulder, he read down the column. "It is only a rumour," he said quietly, "worked up into a thrilling story. There may be nothing in it."

"I sincerely hope so," the Bishop sighed.

"All it amounts to is that Mrs Kearny-Pine left Tecos without saying where she was going. Is that strange?"

"More than strange," the Bishop said solemnly. "It is, in fact, well-nigh impossible. If any such untoward event had occurred, you, Mr Carboy, as the family's legal adviser, would have been immediately informed."

"I have been away," Mr Carboy muttered, rubbing his forehead with a large cambric handkerchief. "There may be a wire at the office now. I'll call up. If you care to wait, Bishop, and you, Mr Pierce. You will miss your train, of course."

The Bishop and Hubert Pierce signified their contempt for trains, under the circumstances. Mr Carboy hurried to the nearest telephone booth. They followed and stood waiting.

"Well?" said the Bishop.

Mr Carboy raised his hand, beckoning, hushing. "Come closer," he whispered, throwing anxious glances right and left. "Not a soul must get wind of this. You swear you won't breathe a word of what I say?"

Three heads nodded. "Three telegrams at my office. One from Mrs Kearny-Pine, received soon after I left on my trip up-state. Not of any immediate interest. One sent yesterday by some person in Tecos named Greenough asking if we knew anything of Mrs Kearny-Pine's present whereabouts. A third, received an hour ago, with frightful news. Frightful! I can hardly believe it, and yet..." Mr Carboy paused to groan and wipe his face again.

"Continue, Mr Carboy! Continue!" the Bishop urged. "Let us know the worst!"

"Mrs Kearny-Pine has been kidnapped!"

2

Six o'clock in Tecos on an April day. The sun was well up over the mountain, and since daybreak the early morning sounds of New Mexico had been drifting in to town. Now Tecos itself was waking up.

But in the hotel – the splendid new Blue Santo Hotel – silence still reigned; the comfortable silence that had descended on the previous evening when the last guest passed yawning up the broad staircase and Pedro the porter, half asleep, had banked the wood fires and extinguished the lights. In the hall crumpled newspapers still lurked in corners and cigarette ashes greyed the Navajo rugs; while, in the stately apartment which in an old-fashioned hotel would have been known as the 'ladies' parlour,' fading flowers mingled their petals with the bits of worsted that Mrs Kearny-Pine's embroidery always left on the carpet when that estimable lady went to bed.

Mrs Couch, the proprietress of the hotel, never called this room the parlour; she preferred living room as a cosier term more apt to make her guests feel at home, whether they came from fifty miles away – Mr Plummer and family from Las Rosas, or five hundred – Miss Spingle from Kansas City, or two thousand – Mr John Greenough from Boston. Especially Mr Greenough. There was nothing, from unsalted butter to more bath towels, that Mrs Couch would not do for Mr Greenough.

For Mr Greenough was not only young and good looking, he had arrived at the hotel with such a plethora of easels, stools and canvases that Mrs Couch could anticipate a long stay, and she naturally preferred permanents to transients.

This craving for 'homeliness' had been a thorn in the flesh of Mr Pinnacle, the architect, during the long planning and building of the hotel. Again and again he had been obliged to remind Mrs Couch that if she wanted a hotel in the Spanish style, he must be allowed a free foot.

He was right, of course, the finished product proved it. "Ohs" of admiration came from every guest entering the lofty front door ornamented with the arms of Miguel de Cordoba and a gilded mitre. Admiration swelled to satisfaction as they passed through the vast dim hall, refreshingly shady after seventy miles of desert, and found themselves in the living room, luxurious yet impeccably Spanish. Mrs Couch herself became so thoroughly converted to Mr Pinnacle's ideas that, as she bade him good-bye, she gave him her solemn promise that nothing in the living room should be changed. No jot added or tittle removed for at least six months. But this promise proved more difficult to keep than she had anticipated.

Mr Pinnacle's car had scarcely left the door when Mrs Couch found Pedro the porter at her elbow bearing a message from the servants' quarters. She stared at his solemn face with amazement.

Then she turned and stared through the door of the living room at a carved image that stood on the mantelpiece.

"The Blue Santo" she exclaimed. "The statue of San Miguel. But why under the sun do you think he will bring us bad luck, Pedro?"

"Alvarez says the Blue Santo is not the linage of San Miguel. Alvarez comes from Old Mexico, and he says he has seen images like that one in his home. They are heathen idols," Pedro crossed himself, "not Christian saints, and they bring bad luck."

"But the hotel is named after him. He's in the folder! What's more, I promised Mr Pinnacle I wouldn't change anything in the living room for at least six months."

Pedro only shook his head mournfully.

Mrs Couch sighed. "Very well," she said. "You go tell Alvarez and the others that I'll raise wages five per cent all round, if they will agree to stay. Tell them when Mr Pinnacle's six months is up I'll send the Blue Santo right back to wherever he came from, and get me another one." And Pedro, with an uncertain smile, departed.

But he came back in a few minutes looking more cheerful. They would risk it.

And now on this early April morning two of the six months had gone by. Yet nothing in the living room had been changed, the Blue Santo still stood on the mantelpiece. No misfortune had come to the hotel, and the servants had ceased to worry about him. He stood there, uncompromisingly erect. A figure some three feet tall carved from wood, painted in dim colours, as shapeless as if he had been born in Noah's ark.

His blue robes fell in stiff folds, his fin-like arms were held stiffly before him. The hands were empty, robbed long since of their palm and chalice, but a magnificent crown of silver filigree surmounted the small pinched face with slit eyes that peered sideways as if keeping watch on the door.

The eyes had watched all night, were still watching when the last peal of the Angelus jangled from St. Joseph's tin steeple a block away, the front door slid open, and Pedro came in. He rolled up the rugs ready for Lost Arrow, his Indian helper, to carry out into the patio for a thorough sweeping, emptied the ash trays, blew the smouldering fire to a blaze, and then approached the desk in a far corner of the hall, sacred later in the day to a pale clerk named Miller.

Breakfast time now. Guests came dawdling down the broad stairway, passed on into the dining room and took their places at the little round tables gay with orange coloured linen and amber glass. As the dining room was separated from the hall only by a row of columns and arches, Mr John Greenough, crossing the hall, could see that Miss Rosalie Colbrook, Mrs Kearny-Pine's young cousin, had already finished her grapefruit. Miss Colbrook wore a cream coloured frock and primrose-yellow sweater. Mr Greenough's artist's eye noted with satisfaction this pleasing combination of colour culminating in the deep rich red of Miss Colbrook's hair, and as he took his seat he gave thanks for the hundredth time that he could drink in Miss Colbrook's loveliness with his coffee.

But today his gratitude was short-lived. One of the little waitresses approached Miss Colbrook, her white doeskin boots sliding soundlessly over the polished floor, and whispered. Miss Colbrook frowned. But she rose and strolled away, giving John Greenough a smiling nod as she passed.

It was nearly eleven before Mrs Kearny-Pine, followed by Rosalie Colbrook and her maid, came downstairs. The hall was empty again. Everyone had gone off on some excursion or other. Mrs Kearny-Pine went on into the living room and deposited herself on a monumental sofa draped with Spanish shawls that spread like a many tinted wing from one side of the fireplace. She was a small woman, neither fat nor thin, her colourless face expressionless except for peevish lines around the mouth. Her clothes were unfashionable, but she wore a fine string of pearls. Seated to her satisfaction, she opened a letter Pedro had given her as she came through the hall, read it carelessly, it was very short and tossed it into the fire.

"Cousin Steve all right?" Rosalie asked perfunctorily.

"Oh, yes. He spent last Sunday with the Barkers at Cold Spring Harbour. You may go, Marie."

The maid departed. Mrs Kearny-Pine opened a work bag, drew out a piece of canvas and began on her needlepoint. Rosalie sat perched on the arm of a chair, smoking cigarettes, tossing half smoked butts and matches into the embers. At length, "It's a heavenly day," she ventured.

"Yes. It is a nice day." Mrs Kearny-Pine hesitated. "A little exercise might be good for me."

Rosalie was already on her feet. "Where shall we go?"

"Let's take a car to that canyon beyond the Rancho that Mr Greenough was telling us about – Canyon del Oro – we might have lunch there."

"Eating out of doors is not my idea of pleasure," Mrs Kearny-Pine said firmly, "and upsetting to the digestion. No, I shall go to the curio shop. I want to get an image like that one up there on the mantelpiece."

"I offered Mrs Couch a hundred and fifty for that figure, but she said she did not wish to part with it at present, not for several months. Of course I won't wait that long."

"Why do you want him? He has a hideous little face."

"I heard before I left home that these images were the latest fashion and I want this one because he's blue – exactly the shade of my drawing room curtains."

A bell rang as they opened the door of the curio shop and went in, but no one answered. A few images and holy pictures hung on the walls among Navajo blankets and beaded doeskin robes, but there were no Blue Santos and Mrs Kearny-Pine was retreating impatiently towards the door when Mr Crowder the proprietor came in from the rear.

Mrs Kearny-Pine explained. He nodded. Yes, he knew the image in the hotel... No, he didn't have one like it, although his was the largest collection of such articles to be found in the Southwest. He ushered them into a dim little inner room, crowded from floor to ceiling with grotesque figures and holy pictures. No, in answer to a suggestion, Mr Crowder said he couldn't even order a Blue Santo for Mrs Kearny-Pine. No, not at any price. The Mexican Penitent, or whoever the carver might have been, had been dead for many a year now and the colour and patina she so admired were lost arts. Indeed that particular 'Santo' was not only unique, it had characteristics very puzzling to an antiquarian.

"Show me the little man up there in the glass case next to the crucifix," Mrs Kearny-Pine broke in. "The one with the sheep. Don't you think he's sort of cute, Rosalie?"

Rosalie nodded, smiling. Mr Crowder mounted a ladder, unhooked a small shrine of perforated tin from near the ceiling, and set it before them. "San Isidro, patron saint of farmers," Mr

Crowder explained.

Mrs Kearny-Pine hesitated. But Rosalie, tired of the stuffy curio shop, praised San Isidro extravagantly. She reminded Cousin Louisa that it was nearly lunch time.

But Mrs Kearny-Pine was not hungry. She went on examining and criticizing, until a tinkle of the doorbell summoned Mr Crowder and the two ladies followed him.

A rough-looking man was turning over the toys on the counter. He drew back, murmuring that his business could wait until Mr Crowder was disengaged, and the discussion was resumed. At length San Isidro was decided upon as being next best to the Blue Santo, and Mrs Kearny-Pine began haggling over the price.

After the dim shop the glare outside was overpowering. Mrs Kearny-Pine raised her parasol, panting, and walked so slowly that Rosalie very nearly let out the scream always near the surface when she was with that lady. The Angelus jangled as they reached the hotel.

"Why, it's only twelve o'clock now, Rosalie!" Mrs Kearny-Pine stopped short. "I don't want to go in just yet. We have plenty of time to visit Governor Dane's house before lunch. They say it is very interesting. You can actually see the blood-stains on the floor."

Rosalie made a face. "I hate blood and guts, and I know that house is just reeking." But she walked on just the same, poor relations usually do.

They came to a low doorway in an adobe hut plastered with a sign: "Governor Dane's House." A Mexican woman sat on the step. She rose smiling, as Mrs Kearny-Pine closed her parasol and prepared to enter. A gush of mouldy dampness came blowing in their faces when the door was opened.

"I'll wait for you outside, Cousin Louisa." Rosalie drew back. "I can't bear that smell of old bones and toadstools." Rosalie stood waiting in the sunlight. The clouds had gone, she noticed discontentedly. John Greenough wouldn't be coming back early after all... She turned with a start.

The door burst open. Mrs Kearny-Pine came hurrying out.

Without waiting to raise her parasol, she clutched Rosalie's sleeve and made for the hotel at a run – a surprisingly fast run very unlike her usual pompous strut – her scarf trailing in the dust. She was very pale.

"What's the matter, Cousin Louisa?" Rosalie cried, as they hurried on. "What happened? Was the woman rude?"

But Cousin Louisa wouldn't, or couldn't, speak until they came in sight of the hotel; and even then she didn't seem to know just what had happened to alarm her. No, the woman hadn't been rude. She had been most polite, had indicated a register to be signed and seemed pleased at getting fifty cents. Then she had opened the door into the 'murder room,' a little dark place like a cellar with nothing in it. Mrs Kearny-Pine had been examining the blood-stains on the floor when a shuffling and whispering began in the entry. Men's voices. She saw them looking at the register, and then they peeped in at her. All of a sudden she felt horribly frightened. There were two men and they stood between her and the front door. But she just took her courage in both hands and nodded good-bye to the woman and brushed past the men with her head up, and they made way for her, and she walked out.

"Perhaps they were talking about your pearls," Rosalie suggested.

"You know Cousin Steve has often warned you not to wear your pearls in queer places like that."

Mrs Kearny-Pine stood still in the middle of the road. "My pearls!" She breathed a sigh of relief. "That must have been it! Those wretches were planning to rob me. Somehow I had a feeling that they were planning something worse than just stealing!" She shuddered, and walked on into the hotel. "Come upstairs with me, Rosalie. I-I don't want to be left alone."

Rosalie had never seen her cousin so gone to pieces. "Marie had better give you some aromatic ammonia," she said pityingly.

"You'll feel ever so much better after a nap."

"A nap! I need more than a nap to make me forget that horrid 'murder house.' I shall take a sleeping powder and stay in bed all the afternoon. I don't want any lunch. My heart feels very queer. A mere nap won't get it back to normal."

Mrs Kearny-Pine was right. A nap was not enough. At dinner time her heart was still fluttering. She dined in bed. At half-past nine Marie administered another sleeping powder and left her mistress for the night.

The sedative worked. Mrs Kearny-Pine slept soundly until St. Joseph's clock rang out the first stroke of midnight. Then she stirred and awoke.

"Marie! Marie!" she called.

There was no answer from the adjoining room where the maid slept, the door half shut. She called again. Still no answer. Mrs Kearny-Pine was annoyed. At length a desire to scold Marie induced action. She rose, put on slippers and dressing gown, and pushed open the door of the next room with an impatient: "Marie, I have called you twice!"

Again there was no answer. She went in, switched on the light and peered inquiringly at Marie, fast asleep in bed. Then she advanced to the bedside and gave the inert figure a reluctant poke. Marie did not move. With a scream of horror, Mrs Kearny-Pine flew to the bell and pressed it again and again. She had known, as soon as she touched her, that Marie was dead! In a moment the room was full of people. Antonio the night watchman was first on the scene; then came Pedro, putting on his coat. Other servants followed. Rosalie ran in, rubbing her eyes like a sleepy child.

Miss Spingle's door opened. Her room was opposite. Other doors opened and guests were peering out all along the corridor, asking what the matter was, when Mrs Couch hurried into the room, wrapped in a shawl, her hair flying, but with all her wits about her.

She realized the situation at once and took charge. Pedro was despatched for the doctor. Rosalie was advised to take the shivering Mrs Kearny-Pine away and put her to bed. Miss Spingle was reassured.

Antonio was sent to calm the other guests. At length the room was clear, and Mrs Couch was standing looking down at the dead face when a voice behind her said quietly: "Can I be of any assistance?"

"Miss Gryce!" Mrs Couch exclaimed. "You are just the person I want. Come here and take a look at this poor soul." Miss Gryce, a neat figure fully dressed in the uniform of a trained nurse, advanced composedly, bent over the body, felt the wrist, raised one of the heavy eyelids, nodded, glanced at a stand beside the bed, nodded again.

"She's dead all right. Probably took an overdose of some sleeping medicine. This is it, I guess." The nurse picked up a bottle that stood beside an empty tumbler on a stand near the bed. " 'Somnola'," she read aloud. "Yes, this is it. I wonder how much -" She broke off as Mrs Kearny-Pine's door opened and Rosalie came in.

"My cousin sent for the jewel case," she said. "Marie kept it at night." Averting her eyes from the bed, she took a blue morocco case from the stand and turned to go.

"Better look inside and make sure that everything is all right," Mrs Couch remarked.

Rosalie obeyed. "The pearls are here," she said, and hurried away.

A moment later footsteps sounded in the corridor, and Pedro ushered in a small man whom Mrs Couch greeted with relief and introduced to Miss Gryce as Dr Sylvestro.

Next morning the hotel awoke earlier than usual and few guests breakfasted in bed, for everybody wanted to hear all about the unfortunate occurrence of the night. By nine o'clock the hall was crowded with guests waiting for Mrs Couch to appear and satisfy their curiosity.

But although Mrs Couch was evidently willing to talk and gratify curiosity to any extent, her story proved disappointing. There was, it appeared, no mystery in the affair and therefore no drama. Not even suicide, according to Dr Sylvestro, merely an unfortunate accident.

Marie had taken an overdose of 'Somnola,' a sleeping medicine with morphine in it. This conclusion was too final to bring more than a perfunctory, "Sad, very sad," from her audience, and Mrs Couch was turning away when Mrs Rowe detained her to ask "And how is dear Mrs Kearny-Pine? This must be a dreadful shock. I hope she is bearing up?"

"Oh, she's bearing up all right," Mrs Couch said drily. "But she doesn't know how she is going to manage without a maid. She says she will have to return to New York if I can't find one for her, and —"

"I have an idea," Miss Clara Burleigh broke in. "Mrs Kearny-Pine might take Miss Gryce off my hands. My health has improved so much in this bracing climate that I don't need a trained nurse, and I was thinking of letting Miss Gryce go when her week was up."

"Miss Gryce is not a lady's maid," Mrs Couch remarked.

"No, but she is so sensible that she might be willing to undertake some of the duties usually assumed by a maid."

Mrs Couch agreed, and went upstairs to make the suggestion to Mrs Kearny-Pine. It was well received. Miss Gryce was summoned.

She proved as sensible as Miss Burleigh had prophesied. She was engaged.

"Every cloud has a silver lining," Mrs Kearny-Pine remarked to Rosalie, as Miss Gryce left the room to collect her belongings. "Perhaps it is all for the best. Marie was getting old and I really need a trained nurse after the shocks I have had." She shivered. "First that horrid fright in the 'murder house,' and then Marie! I still feel quite upset. I have a sense of insecurity, of danger."

Rosalie regarded her cousin's worried little face with concern. "Would you like Cousin Steve to come?" she asked.

"Steve?" Mrs Kearny-Pine hesitated. "Stephen is very wearing, he is so exuberant. Though it might be a good idea. After all, he is a man and it would be a comfort to feel there was a man around. Give me a telegraph form."

Rosalie complied. A message was written and despatched.

3

Janet Gryce found her new duties easy enough and fatiguing only to the spirit. Like most nurses, she preferred a case of serious illness.

But she had no wish to return to the East just yet. She managed to get through Mrs Kearny-Pine's morning routine without arousing more than perfunctory reproof, and eleven o'clock saw that lady safely deposited in the living room. The tray was brought to her, glanced at, handed to Miss Gryce to take upstairs and the latter was dismissed. If Mrs Kearny-Pine needed anything, Miss Colbrook would see to it.

Miss Gryce did not glance at the letters she was carrying until she reached her own room and the return address on an envelope happened to catch her eye. She started as if she had been shot, hurried to the window, snapped up the shade, and looked again at the envelope. Her full lips compressed, she stood staring, the colour slowly seeping from her face.

" 'Society for the Nourishment of Infant Paupers,' " she muttered. "Now why in hell are they writing to Mrs Kearny-Pine?"

Miss Gryce rolled a pencil under the flap of the envelope and drew out a sheet of paper. There at the top the name of Mrs Kearny-Pine appeared as second vice-president! That was bad, even worse than she had feared. She ran her eye down the typewritten page: "New cases... Cases pending... Cases terminated." and came to the last paragraph:

"Regret to inform you that investigation following the recent resignation of Miss Jane Greer, one of our most trusted nurses, discloses a most distressing state of affairs. Miss Greer appears to have embezzled a considerable sum of money during the months she has been in the employment of the Society. Her present whereabouts are as yet unknown. We shall, of course, keep you informed of later developments."

Miss Gryce stood absently folding the paper into smaller and smaller squares. What was to be done? Destroy the letter? Or risk letting Mrs Kearny-Pine read it? Would Mrs K.P. in any way connect the absconding Jane Greer with Janet Gryce, the nurse she had just engaged? It was not likely, but it was safer to take no chances. Miss Gryce tore the letter into small scraps and effectually disposed of the remains in the adjoining bathroom.

Then she sank limply into a chair by the window. But as she sat staring down into the sunlit street, four walls suddenly became unbearable. She jammed on a hat, dashed downstairs, out into the open air, and without looking where she was going, turned into a high road over-arched by giant poplars. As she hurried on, looking neither to right nor left, she felt pursued. Pursued by the last six months, months that had seemed safely buried but were now rising from the dead. Months that, as she looked back at them, seemed horribly striped with black and white.

How had it all begun? Was it the night at the 'Mouse Trap' when Buck and Rita – Rita in a new dress – had gone dancing away from her? Or was it the week at Atlantic City later on, when Rita could afford to stay at the hotel that Buck liked and she, Jane, couldn't? Or was it...? Oh, what was the use of settling when and how and where it had begun? She needed money if she expected to keep up with Buck, any charitable society as mean to their employees as the 'Infant Paupers' was deserved to be cheated. Anyway, it had been a clever idea. Even now, Janet Gryce, walking along the dusty road, tossed her head, smiling at the cleverness of the idea.

And, at first, it had seemed no more than a good joke. Each time that Jane Greer turned in her report to the superintendent of the cases she had visited during the week – so much spent for milk, so much for eggs, so much for garments – she had slipped in one new pauper family of her own invention, such as:

"Messagio, Angelo. 67 Cornelia Street. Six children. Father

longshoreman, out of work. Mother drinks. Angelo, aged four, T.B. Should go to Sea Breeze but parents refuse. But willing to accept two quarts of milk and six eggs daily. Will visit frequently and make every effort to influence family."

Once embarked on this course of short-story writing, how smoothly everything had gone! As she happened to be the only visiting nurse employed by the Society on the lower West Side, she was free to invent any number of shiftless families in that district, to discover dozens of undernourished Angelos and Patricks and Isaacs, to run up her weekly account for milk and eggs by adding more expensive articles, spectacles for near-sighted 'Infant Paupers', paint-boxes for the artistic, sewing materials for little 'shut-ins'. She often ran it up to the tune of ten or fifteen dollars a week. The Society being rich and incompetent, Miss Greer's activity was considered most commendable.

And how pleasantly and profitably that ten or fifteen dollars a week had been spent! Rita had vanished. Buck had stayed.

But of course it was too good to last. Janet shivered, walking along the hot dusty road, remembering that winter morning a few short weeks ago when, coming unexpectedly into the office, she had found Miss Jones the superintendent examining a record card with a puzzled frown.

Miss Jones had looked up inquiringly.

"Have the Messagios moved since Wednesday?" she had asked. "I happened to be going through Cornelia Street yesterday afternoon, and I thought I would stop in and see if I could persuade the mother to let little Angelo go to Sea Breeze. But there was no such family living at 67. No Italians, in fact, in that tenement."

Jane had kept her head. "Oh, I'm so sorry – so ashamed," she cried. "Of course, it isn't the Messagios who live in Cornelia Street, it's the Reillys. You see they have the same number, number 67, and I got the streets mixed on the cards. So careless of me. I'm so sorry you had that trip for nothing, Miss Jones. Couldn't you go again some other day? 67 Bank Street is the right address. They're the slackest, dirtiest family I ever knew, and you are so experienced and so kind. And little Angelo is the sweetest kid, such big dark eyes."

In the end, Miss Jones had accepted her apology. But Jane Greer, listening humbly to a lecture on the sacredness of vital statistics in general and of office records in particular, became sickeningly aware that the superintendent was not entirely satisfied. As she left the office, Miss Jones was already examining other cards bearing inscriptions in Miss Greer's neat handwriting, describing other cases even more interesting than that of Angelo Messagio, too interesting, in fact. When Miss Jones got to the last card, the Einstein's, father Italian, mother Irish, five undernourished infants, some of them cripples needing spectacles, others myopic needing braces, and a lot more nonsense written in a tearing hurry because Buck was waiting in the street, the jig, Miss Greer told herself, was undoubtedly up. And acted accordingly.

Regardless of expense, she took a taxi all the way to her boarding house in the Bronx, paid the landlady, explaining that she had just heard her mother was dying in Buffalo, packed the two dress suitcases that held her clothes, very pretty clothes, thanks to the fictitious 'Infant Paupers', stepped into another taxi and into another world. In that taxi Miss Jane Greer ceased to exist and from it Miss Janet Gryce emerged like a handsome butterfly from a dingy chrysalis.

Within a few hours she had acquired a new haircut that altered her considerably, and that evening in the privacy of another hall bedroom – in Greenwich Village, but otherwise much like her last – she darkened and sleeked her fluffy blonde coiffure, and added a brunette make-up which she rather liked and hoped that Buck would also approve.

Unlucky Buck wasn't in town and couldn't be consulted. He had gone to Montreal on something connected with business – just what that business was Jane Greer had never inquired and Janet Gryce would be equally discreet. She was obliged to content herself with writing to the general post office in Montreal, presenting a humorous account of the break with the 'Infant Paupers' and her interview with Miss Jones, and imploring him to write at once to the New York post office, where she would leave a forwarding address.

But he had not written! Why hadn't he written? Perhaps he was sick. Perhaps he was dead. Perhaps he had found another girl. It would be weeks before she could save enough of her salary to buy a ticket to Canada, and by that time – Janet had no illusions about her young man – even if Buck wasn't either ill or dead, he would most certainly have found another girl!

Now, walking along the high road, disheartened by this gloomy conclusion, Janet's feet dragged. As the road narrowed to a lane she suddenly found herself overcome by fatigue and sat down on a grassy bank to rest. It was an uninteresting spot. But she was too lazy to move and sat staring down at the dusty grass at her feet until a clop clop of horses' hooves broke the silence and a man came riding by.

It was an Indian; an Indian from the Pueblo. The horse was a big grey animal, larger and better cared for than the run of Indian horses, and six or eight dogs snapped and scampered at his heels, dogs of many breeds and colours but all mongrel and all small.

Janet Gryce recognized the rider. He was James Rio from the Pueblo. She rose mechanically and walked on until, rounding a curve in the lane, she came face to face with the Pueblo.

In the centre of a wide open space of hard-trodden, sun-baked ground as flat and clean as a threshing floor, a castle like structure built up of set-back rectangles terraced and piled one upon another like a modern apartment house, rose majestically, its six or seven storeys giving the effect of far greater height. The base, like that of a medieval castle, was clustered with humbler excrescences, thatched shelters for cattle, hen houses, round topped ovens. And the whole seemed strangely to reflect the weather, as if the place had an affinity with nature.

Today was sunny. The Pueblo flashed with colour and was alive with sound. Dogs, chickens and children, barking, cackling, laughing and crying. Women in bright blankets, carrying earthen jars, ran up and down ladders that led to the upper stories. For a moment Janet, standing unobserved, caught a glimpse of the real Pueblo. Not the grim, apathetic face it kept for tourists, never welcome in spite of the money they brought in.

But it was only for a moment. As her white clad figure appeared on the farther side of the stream half encircling the open space around the village, and advanced to the single bridge of logs that was the Pueblo's front door, stillness fell and colour vanished as if she had shown the Gorgon's head. Women and children scuttled under cover like rabbits. The men stopped their game and stood watching Miss Gryce as she paused, hesitating whether or not to cross the bridge, for that silent gaze was terrifying.

She was turning away when a scream came from a boy sitting beside the brook. He raised a bleeding hand and her nurse's instinct took her running across the bridge.

"It's a bad cut." She looked up at the men who now stood uncertainly about, and began winding her handkerchief around the boy's wrist. But before she could get the bandage knotted, women came running and shrieking from all directions. One of them snatched the boy up in her arms and tried to drag him away. The bandage loosened, blood gushed out. The woman dabbed at it with the corner of her filthy shawl and screamed louder.

"Take care," the nurse cried. "He'll bleed to death!" She held on to the bandage. Both women struggled for possession of the boy who was yelling at the top of his voice. The men seemed unwilling to interfere.

Miss Gryce was about to give up in despair, when a shout rang out. A horse came cantering up the lane, leaped the stream, and the rider, James Rio, flung himself out of the saddle and joined the mêlée.

"What has happened?" he asked in English, motioning the

women to stand back and addressing himself to Miss Gryce, already intent on readjusting her bandage. "How did he hurt himself?"

"He cut his wrist with that knife. Not badly, but it's a rusty old thing." She pointed to a broken-bladed knife that lay on the ground.

"And that woman wanted to wipe the blood with a filthy rag. I'm a trained nurse. I'll dress the wound properly if you can get me some disinfectant – salt and water will do if you haven't anything better – and a strip of clean cloth. It will soon heal."

James Rio nodded. "He is my son," he remarked, and without noticing the women in any way, he bent over the boy, lifted him in his arms and walked across the yard to the main building of the Pueblo, Miss Gryce holding the wrist in a firm clasp. He bent his head at a low doorway, entered a small whitewashed room and laid the boy on a bench.

"I will send for iodine," he said. "We have iodine and everything necessary."

The room had no windows except a small square hole in one wall, opening into the next room and plugged with a little pillow. As they came in the pillow was withdrawn, a woman's face appeared in the aperture. She listened meekly to the man's directions, and turned to obey.

Miss Gryce glanced curiously about the little room. It was as white and specklessly clean as a convent parlour; even the long low bench on which the boy lay was covered with a white sheet. The only colour was a row of small pictures pinned on the walls, all pictures of the Pueblo, from various points of view and painted at different seasons of the year.

James Rio gave a grunt of satisfaction as he saw her eye rest on the pictures. "My work," he said proudly, waving his hand. "I am an artist. I make pictures. I sell my pictures for three dollars apiece."

"What lovely work!" Her admiration and surprise were

genuine. "You must enjoy it ever so much."

"A brush is less heavy to hold than a shovel…" He broke off. "Here is the iodine."

Two women came in: a very ancient woman with a face like a shrivelled raisin, wrapped in a black shawl, carrying towels and a basin of water; and a young girl in pink gingham, with a medicine bottle, boxes of gauze and absorbent cotton, adhesive tape – everything necessary, as James Rio had promised.

At length the arm lay in a neat white cocoon. "He'll be all right now." Janet Gryce rose and glanced at her watch. "Oh, dear!" she cried. "I must hurry, or I'll be late for lunch at the hotel. It's after one and –"

James Rio broke in politely. "I am grateful to you. It was fortunate for my family that you were here when my boy Peter hurt himself."

"You're quite welcome I'm sure." She turned hastily to the door.

Again he interposed, waving his hand towards the wall. "I will give you a present. I will give you one of my pictures. You may choose. Take whichever picture you like best."

"Oh, thank you. How very kind." She indicated one of the sketches at random. "I'd love to have that one. I really must be going," she insisted. "It's quite a long walk and –"

"You do not have to walk. I have a Ford. I will send you back to the hotel in my Ford."

Thanks to the Ford, Miss Gryce reached the hotel with a few minutes to spare. But the living room was empty and she hurried upstairs to Mrs Kearny-Pine's room.

"So here you are at last," that lady said grimly. She was lying on the bed, flat on her back, Rosalie hovering in the background. "I couldn't imagine what had become of you. I think I am going to have a heart attack. Get me my drops at once. And a hot water bag. And a fan. And draw down the shades, can't you see that the glare is hurting my eyes? Rosalie, don't stand staring at me. Go down and have your lunch. Tell them to send me some hot milk. Hot.

But not boiled."

Rosalie tiptoed away. Murmuring sympathetically, Miss Gryce moved about the room; administering drops, manipulating the window shades to the exact point demanded by her patient. Mrs Kearny-Pine closed her eyes.

At length Mrs Kearny-Pine decided to take a nap. Janet was dismissed. Leaving the door of the room ajar, she knocked at Rosalie Colbrook's door and went in.

"How is she?" Rosalie asked, without turning from the looking glass where she was trying on a pale yellow hat.

"Not so good. It isn't a heart attack. Her heart's all right for the time being. But she seems terribly nervous. What's that?"

A long shuddering scream rang down the corridor. Miss Gryce flew back to her patient's room, followed by Rosalie.

Mrs Kearny-Pine was sitting bolt upright, eyes popping in a dead white face, hands clutching the sheet. "Something grabbed at me from under the bed!" she gabbled. "Something reached out from under the bed and grabbed at me. There's something awful under the bed..."

Miss Gryce bent and looked under the bed. "Nothing there but your slippers," she said calmly. "I guess you had a nightmare, Mrs Kearny-Pine. Lie down again, and I'll fan you."

"But I tell you I wasn't asleep," the lady cried indignantly. "I had woken up. Then I felt – I knew – something was coming out from under the bed, and I screamed. Don't stand there like logs – search! The thing may be here still hiding. In the clothes closet – in the bathroom..."

Miss Gryce and Rosalie ran about obediently, looking in every possible and impossible place where something awful and bad smelling could have hidden itself. But there was nothing to be found. At length Mrs Kearny-Pine lay down again, acknowledging with a sigh of exhaustion that she must after all have been dreaming.

4

Stephen Pine was sitting in a compartment of the Twentieth Century Limited, grudging every turn of the wheels that drew him farther and farther from the city, smoking sulkily and all by himself. Stephen Pine was both gregarious and garrulous. But today he wanted to be alone, to think and to remember. He shut his eyes, trying to recover every detail of that Long Island Sunday two weeks ago.

When he arrived at the Barkers' he had been ushered straight out on the terrace. Everybody was having tea. Many people he knew and a few he didn't. Among the latter was a girl sitting on the balustrade, one sleek leg dangling. Her name, it turned out, was Mrs Larkin. Divorced, of course – no woman with a figure like that would be content with one experiment. She had made room for him on her perch. They had enjoyed a few cocktails together, played tennis together until dinner time, danced afterwards. Next day he had driven her back to town in his car. And all through, they had talked, discovered in each other the most remarkable similarities of mind and heart. Never had a friendship ripened so fast. This very night he was to have dined with Mrs Larkin – Arabella.

But the fates – and Louisa – had decreed otherwise. Here he was in a dingy coop smelling of cinders with not even a decent meal to look forward to... A harsh-voiced waiter drifted down the aisle: "Last call for dinner." Dinner indeed! And a restless night to follow. Then some more of both. He hadn't taken the trouble to find out just how long it took to get to Tepos – or Tecos – or whatever its godforsaken name was. A thousand miles anyway. He gnashed his large white teeth. Louisa would get a piece of his mind for once. Louisa must be made to understand that he, Stephen Pine, was a husband and not a slave skulking to heel at the lift of her finger. Other women didn't treat him like a dog. Mrs Larkin – Arabella – didn't despise him. Far from it. Arabella-Arabella-Arabella. The grinding wheels became almost musical, keeping time to that charming name.

But even a love sick man – Steve frankly acknowledged his deplorable condition – must eat if he wishes to return to the arms of his beloved, and this he had every intention of doing as rapidly as possible. He followed the harsh-voiced waiter. The head waiter immediately discerned Steve's handsome presence, plucked him out of the rabble and seated him at a table for two where a young man in clerical dress was consuming a baked apple.

Steve didn't much like clergymen, but he had been educated at St. Paul's and was always polite to the 'cloth'. He nodded. In a few minutes the two were chatting and had exchanged names.

Oddly enough, their destinations proved to be the same. The Reverend Samuel Wurtz was also on his way to Tecos. His health, he explained, having been impaired by a too strict attention to duty, his congregation had made up a purse and sent him West to recuperate. He proposed to stop over in Santa Fe only long enough to see the cathedral and proceed by stage to Tecos seventy miles farther on.

"Stage?" Steve put in carelessly as he pushed back his chair. "You say it's seventy miles? Mountain roads too, of course. I don't hold with stages. I'll get a car in Santa Fe and give you a lift."

The Reverend Samuel was fulsomely grateful. Steve cut him short. But the little fellow was better than nobody and Steve had done enough thinking and remembering for the present. "Come along back with me," he said, as they left the dining car. "I've got some good cigars."

The clergyman proved appreciative of a good cigar, and though he declined the spot of something that Stephen offered as an accompaniment, he concealed whatever professional disapprobation he may have felt as Stephen refreshed himself, and proved such a sympathetic listener that Stephen, becoming mellow, talked with less and less restraint, and by the time the train reached Rochester, had embarked on an inventory of Arabella's charms.

But when Stephen hinted at the inconvenience of being saddled with a wife, he met with rebuke.

"Whom God hath joined together," Mr Wurtz reminded him, "let no man put asunder."

Steve yawned. "You talk just like Louisa. Louisa isn't going to loosen that knot this side of heaven. And that's where I wish she was now," he added viciously. "Dead and buried and gone to heaven and a nice tombstone to keep her down."

Next day, however, after a good lunch in Chicago, Stephen Pine's spirits rose. He was amused to find his compartment on the Santa Fe road supplied with many novel gadgets and had begun unpacking by the simple process of turning his bag upside down on the sofa, when Mr Wurtz appeared in the door, on his way, he explained, to the observation car.

"I'll join you in a minute," Stephen nodded cheerfully, flinging garments about with a recklessness that would have distressed his valet.

"Keep a seat for me on the platform. It promises to be a fine day."

"Dear me! I hope that isn't loaded," the clergyman exclaimed, as Steve tossed a small revolver on top of some shirts. "Do you always carry a gun?"

Steve laughed. "My man's idea. Egbert is English and I suppose he thinks firearms necessary for a Wild West outfit."

Mr Wurtz smiled and passed on. Steve was about to follow, when the door of the adjoining compartment opened in answer to a knock from a maid standing in the aisle. He heard a voice say, "Come in!" and stood transfixed. He would know that voice among a thousand – it was the voice of Arabella!

As the maid departed, Steve sprang out into the aisle. The door of the next compartment was still open. A woman stood inside with her back turned, unpacking.

"Arabella" he cried. "Arabella – is it really you?"

She turned, let the dress fall to the floor. "Steve!" she exclaimed in equal astonishment.

They stood gazing for a second, then both began talking at once.

"Didn't you get my message yesterday?"

"Message? What message?"

"That I couldn't dine with you, of course."

"Why, that's the message I sent *you*..."

Finally, the strange, and utterly enchanting coincidence became clear. Both of them had been summoned to the West in a hurry, both had departed reluctantly. She to the sick bed of an aged and pernicious aunt in Santa Barbara; he to what he sincerely hoped was the sick bed of an inconvenient wife in New Mexico.

When, a few minutes later, having been delayed by a chat with the conductor, Mr Wurtz approached the rear platform, he found his new friend Mr Pine already there, but so engrossed by the conversation of the pretty lady who sat beside him that the reverend man judged it more discreet to withdraw for the present. And the second day passed for all three travellers in much the same manner.

At length prairie gave way to desert, pale mountains appeared on the horizon. The inevitable moment of parting for Steve and Arabella was here.

The train slowed down for the junction at Lamy. Passengers for Santa Fe jammed themselves into the narrow exits in accordance with the Pullman Company's eccentric method of debarkation. The Reverend Mr Wurtz found himself standing directly behind the pretty lady to whom Mr Pine seemed so attached. She had no hat on her curly head, obviously she was not leaving the train. She stood pressed close to Mr Pine in front of her, closer than even the Pullman Company considers necessary. The couple murmured together in a mournful undertone.

"We're helpless," the lady moaned. "There's no way out."

"I'll force a way!" Mr Pine hissed fiercely. "If Louisa won't listen to reason it will be the worse for her I tell you, I'll do anything – *anything* – to get free!"

The train crashed to a nerve-racking stop. The porter went leaping back and forth like a chamois among the piled up luggage. Arabella raised her face for a last kiss, turned away sobbing.

The two men patronized different hotels in Santa Fe and did not meet again that night. But Mr Wurtz had no intention of losing the free and comfortable transportation to Tecos that had been promised him, so he contrived to run across Stephen Pine in the street as he came out after a late breakfast. A cheerful "Good morning," followed by an allusion to the Tecos stage, brought the desired invitation.

5

Meanwhile, Mrs Kearny-Pine was recovering from her attack of nerves. But she still felt disinclined for festivity, and Rosalie dressed for Algy Atwater's cocktail party and came downstairs in a carefree mood.

Through the archway into the dining room she could see John Greenough still at lunch – he had come in very late. Rosalie sat down by the hall fire, lighted a cigarette and gave the dining room the full benefit of her profile. John Greenough instantly flung down his napkin and bounded to his feet.

She smiled with satisfaction – she was only eighteen. Fishing was pretty good fun when the only bait you needed was your own profile! As he joined her beside the fire, Bella came by on her way upstairs with a tray. Bella was the prettiest of the three pretty little Indian waitresses, whose costume – full-skirted, high-waisted cotton frocks, each a different colour, beaded belts and white doeskin boots – added such a charming picturesqueness to the dining room.

"Isn't Bella sweet in pink!" Rosalie remarked.

"She's very pretty. But she has a sad little face. I wonder why."

"I know why. She's crossed in love. Bella and I are great friends. She's told me all about it. Her young man belongs to a tribe that isn't received in Pueblo society. She met him here at the hotel and if she won't give him up she will have to come back to the Pueblo where they can keep an eye on her. The poor little thing doesn't know what to do. Isn't it hard luck!"

John Greenough agreed that Bella's predicament was decidedly uncomfortable, and agreed with still more enthusiasm when Rosalie suggested his going with her to Algy Atwater's party. He ran upstairs two steps at a time.

"Quick change," she said approvingly as he reappeared – he now presented the glistening effect of a man who has taken a bath, shaved and had his hair cut. I do like yellow hair and a perfect sunburn, Rosalie said to herself, as they went out into the street.

"Algy must have perpetrated another masterpiece, or he wouldn't be throwing a party," John Greenough remarked. "At its best, my vocabulary of praise is inadequate, and when Algy presents his latest offspring I am 'stricken dumb,' like Balaam."

"Poor Algy. But he doesn't expect much. Everybody just mutters and looks the other way. And his rum swizzle's are all right."

They skirted the plaza, and turned into a narrow, dark, crooked little alley that took them by twists and angles to a green door guarded by the stone face of a Mexican god protruding angrily from a wall of pink stucco.

The door stood ajar. From within came an agreeable clatter of teacups and glasses, laughter and talk. Some twenty people were scattered about the large high-ceilinged room. It was a studio like any one of a dozen studios in Tecos, with slight variations.

Algy Atwater nodded at Rosalie and John Greenough as they came in, from a side table where he was languidly shaking cocktails. At the moment, Miss Joy had the floor and was explaining to the two Miss Burleighs just why it was that a painter who specialized in nudes and palm trees should plant her easel in a land of war bonnets and cactus.

Miss Joy, it appeared, liked Tecos because of the atmosphere.

"It's this way, Professor!" – the Miss Burleighs had wandered to another part of the room, and only Professor Bridges, the well known botanist, author of *Rusts and Moulds of the Pacific Slope*, was left as an audience. "It's this way. Nowhere in the world does one dream as one dreams in Tecos! For nowhere, not even in Madagascar, does one breathe an atmosphere so impregnated with a sort of divine cruelty. Emanations, Professor! Emanations! From the Pueblo Indians? From the Penitentes? Who shall say? But my Tecos nights are rich with dreams; dreams so utterly Freudian that

I wake up just screaming with delight."

But the Professor was not interested in Freud or in art, and sat absently sipping his tea until Miss Joy paused to reach for another cocktail and a demure voice at his elbow brought him back to the present scene. It was Miss Spingle, the Kansas school teacher.

"You grow orchids, I believe," she murmured deferentially, "and have had extraordinary success with hybridization. How I wish I could wander through your conservatories!"

The Professor's face brightened, his mouth opened, but before he could get out a word, Miss Joy broke in:

"Orchids! So you grow orchids, Professor, such wicked flowers! Its aura is malevolent. What do you say, Professor? Isn't an orchid evil *in itself*?" But again the Professor only stared at her in silence, and she was obliged to turn to Mr Magilp:

"All I need is a stimulant for my subconscious. My subconscious..."

But Mr Magilp moved relentlessly away – Miss Joy's subconscious was an old old story – and sat down beside Rosalie.

"I can't stand Julia Joy," he began, and broke off. Algy had rolled his easel forward and was demanding admiration for a six-by-four canvas.

For a moment no one spoke. Then old Mrs Rowe moved nearer, peered through her spectacles, let out a small squeak: "Oh my goodness!" and went shuddering back to her chair; while Algy, radiating satisfaction, embarked on an explanation of his new technique, cut short, to everybody's relief, by Miss Joy.

"Good God, Algy!" she snorted, her broad pale face reddening with anger. "You ought to be spanked! How dare you attempt to paint the glorious horrors of a Penitent procession when you've never ventured within a mile of one? Why, you'd run like a deer, if you –"

But a universal murmur of protest drowned her voice. Mr Magilp remarked on "a bit of nice brushwork in the middle distance," Miss Clara Burleigh asked for another cup of tea. Algy wheeled the easel back into its corner. Everybody wanted to forget Algy's picture as soon as possible. Algy didn't really care. He knew damn well he couldn't paint. But it pleased Aunt Louisa to think he could and it was a lot more fun than selling bonds or real estate.

Miss Spingle, having modestly refrained from criticizing Algy's work, now ventured to address Mr Magilp.

"I don't quite understand that picture of Mr Atwater's," she breathed.

"Why did Miss Joy say Mr Atwater would 'run like a deer' if be met a Penitent procession? Are those Penitentes *dangerous*, Mr Magilp?"

"No indeed," be said soothingly. "But I wouldn't go wandering about alone on the Mountain until after Easter, Miss Spingle. The Penitentes have peculiar ways of expiating their sins during Lent and you might see something pretty unpleasant." He sighed and went on, to Rosalie: "I thought Mrs Kearny-Pine would be here today." And sighed again when Rosalie explained that her cousin wasn't feeling very well: Mr Magilp would not have wasted an afternoon in Algy's studio if he hadn't hoped to meet Algy's aunt. As a possible patron of the arts, Mrs Kearny-Pine was already very popular in Tecos.

"You say Aunt Louisa isn't feeling well?" Algy put in, taking Mr Magilp's place on the divan as he moved away, and before John Greenough could do so. "Not a heart attack, I suppose?" he ended hopefully.

Lowering her voice, Rosalie told him about the visit to Governor Dane's house and how frightened Cousin Louisa had been.

"I don't understand it," Algy frowned. "The caretakers are relations of James Rio, the fellow that paints those funny little thumbnails of the Pueblo." He broke off, Paquita, the Indian girl, was approaching with her tray. "I haven't found a name for my new dog yet," he went on. The Indian girl moved away. Algy turned to Rosalie.

"I changed the subject," he explained, "because Paquita is a cousin of those caretakers at Governor Dane's house. To go back to what we were saying – it isn't a bit like Aunt Louisa to be frightened. I don't understand it."

"It was probably only the squalid atmosphere that frightened her. And the smell!" Rosalie shuddered. "Why do people go to see that horrid little house, Algy?"

"Governor Dane was murdered there."

'"But you don't go to see a place just because somebody was killed in it – except Rizzio or someone like that."

"Oh, Magilp!" Algy called across the room. "Miss Colbrook wants to know why Governor Dane's house is interesting to the public. You know all about Tecos and its history."

It wasn't so much the murder," Magilp explained, "as the punishment that followed it. The Pueblo had risen and was smashing things right and left when General Kearny got here, but he could have overlooked most of the damage if they hadn't ended by chopping down the Governor in his own house. Kearny, of course, hung the ringleaders, James Rio's grandfather among them. According to the Pueblo, Desert Eagle was innocent, and this may have added romance to the story. Anyway, the 'murder house' has become one of the regular sightseeing places in New Mexico."

"I wonder if it's haunted," Rosalie murmured. "Cousin Louisa said she felt something uncanny about the place. Perhaps she saw a ghost without realizing it."

"A ghost of Governor Dane, or of General Kearny?" Mr Magilp laughed. "By the way, Mrs Kearny-Pine is not a relation of the General's?"

"Oh no. Another family entirely. Cousin Steve despises that hyphen. Cousin Louisa stuck it in after she came back from England the last time."

"I see. Well, Miss Colbrook, I must be going. Tell Mrs Kearny-Pine that I shall hope for a visit from her in my studio one day soon. It's just beyond the *represso* – I understand she is interested in Mexican curios and my collection is worth seeing."

"She'd love to come. Cousin Louisa is simply crazy about those Santos and holy pictures. She's fearfully sunk because Mrs Couch won't sell her that blue one in the hotel. No, thank you, Paquita, no more cake. Have you any like that blue one, Mr Magilp?"

"No, he's unique. And probably exceedingly valuable. I've never examined him myself, but Jonas Train, my cowboy model, knows a lot about curios. He used to live in Old Mexico and he has an interesting theory about that image. He thinks it was originally a Mexican idol, converted into a saint by some pious Christian who carved the head over and painted the face as you see it now. Just how the thing got to Tecos, no one seems to know."

"How marvellous!" Rosalie breathed. "When Cousin Louisa hears your story, she'll get that Blue Santo or die in the attempt." She rose. "Good-bye, Algy. It's been a lovely party."

Algy took both of her hands in his and held them. "Rosalie," he murmured, "you are divine in yellow. Come around tomorrow and I'll paint your portrait – same frock, same hat."

Rosalie hesitated. Algy was rather a worm. However…

"Perhaps." She smiled and strolled out of the studio. John Greenough followed.

Algy stood rubbing his chin reflectively. Greenough was certainly smitten. Radiating lovelorn-ness from every pore. Very, very foolish of Aunt Louisa to let Rosalie run around all over the place with a man she knew nothing about! That is, if Aunt Louisa really wanted her latest matchmaking scheme to go through.

Algy was perfectly aware of Mrs Kearny-Pine's chief reason for visiting Tecos; Aunt Louisa hadn't come to New Mexico merely to find out for herself how her nephew was getting on. She had a more romantic reason. She had brought her two young dependants, Rosalie Colbrook and Algy Atwater, together, hoping they might take a fancy to each other.

Algy turned back into his now empty studio, stretched himself on a divan, piled cushions under his slightly bald head and lay contemplating the tips of his pea-green pumps. And then the memory of the morning's miseries, forgotten for the moment in the bosom of art and society, came washing in again, overwhelming him in a complete maelstrom of wretchedness.

Every single thing that morning had gone wrong, beginning at nine o'clock. His breakfast egg had been too soft, his toast too hard, the honey was 'out'. And then – oh, then – the mail had come! It was the first of the month when you expected the worst, and this morning's mail had not only brought two entirely forgotten bills of monstrous size, but a letter from his dealer. This crescendo of bad news had risen to a scream at the end. That little devil in Los Angeles, Myrtle Cream, had, somehow or other, got hold of Mrs Kearny-Pine's name, realized what that name implied, and was threatening to write to her at once if Algy didn't fork out more liberally than in the past.

Tears stood in Algy's eyes. Pretty hard to keep a stiff upper lip when you were given a mail like that to digest. As usual Algy's only consolation was the thought of Aunt Louisa's heart. If he could hold on a very little longer, Aunt Louisa's heart would bring all his troubles to a satisfactory conclusion – not by softening, but by going obligingly out of business.

It was a matter of common knowledge – Mrs Kearny-Pine being fond of making wills and still fonder of talking about them – that her nephew was to inherit a fourth of the fortune, born in her father's grocery store in Newark, 'the first bright link of an endless chain' that now stretched from coast to coast and threatened to cross the Pacific. The latest edition of Mrs Kearny-Pine's will gave Algy this succulent quarter, her husband a half and Rosalie an eighth; the remaining eighth to be distributed among various pet charities.

So far so good. But Aunt Louisa happened to be incredibly Victorian. Would she understand this Myrtle Cream combination? She would not! In fact, if Aunt Louisa didn't die before she and Los Angeles got connected up, there would be the devil and all to pay and it was "bye-bye, blackbird" with a vengeance!

In the meantime, Rosalie and John Greenough were quarrelling. It had begun by silence on Mr Greenough's part. Rosalie naturally inquired as to its cause, resented the explanation, let herself go in a medley of reasons and excuses. She didn't need to be told that Algy was rather a worm, but Mr Greenough seemed to forget that Algy was also a cousin – that is, sort of. And if Mr Greenough wanted to paint her portrait, why couldn't he have said so sooner? Anyway, it was too late now for she had promised Algy. Or at least, sort of promised. And a girl might be only eighteen, thank you, and yet perfectly capable of taking care of herself...

When they got back to the hotel, Rosalie ran upstairs without so much as a smile and was gone before John Greenough could say Jack Robinson – not that he had any desire to do so. He was entirely too sunk for speech of any sort.

6

Next day Rosalie awoke to a morning of such flawless blue and gold that she went down to breakfast still undecided as to how it should be. Bella came slipping noiselessly to Rosalie's side, and stood waiting.

"What fruits do you wish?" she murmured in a voice as soft as silk.

Rosalie ordered melon, and added a careless: "Mr Greenough has finished his breakfast?"

"Mr Greenough is finish veree earlee today. He tell me he is going to paint in Canyon del Oro. I make him sandwiches."

Canyon del Oro indeed! The mean skunk – hadn't he promised and vowed to take Rosalie along next time he went there? Hadn't he suggested they make a day of it and take their lunch in the cave on the farther side? Rosalie ground her teeth with rage as she finished her last morsel of bacon and eggs, was still raging when she knocked at Mrs Kearny-Pine's door a few minutes later.

That lady was sitting up in bed, with a breakfast tray across her knees. Evidently she was feeling better.

"Algy was so sorry you couldn't come yesterday, Cousin Louisa," Rosalie remarked. "It wasn't so bad, as teas go. Everybody sent you kind messages and said they hoped you'd be better soon."

Mrs Kearny-Pine went on eating, she was accustomed to kind messages. "Algy wants to paint my portrait, Cousin Louisa. Do you think it's worth while to let him try?"

Mrs Kearny-Pine set down her coffee cup. "An excellent idea," she said. "It's very kind of the dear boy to suggest it. Rosalie, you have my permission. Tell Algy to come to tea with me this afternoon."

But this approval failed to dispel Rosalie's doubts. She found herself in an unusually depressed frame of mind as she made her way through Algy's crooked alley to the studio, and Algy's face, looking out at her as he opened the door, seemed even puffier and more unwholesome than usual.

Algy's gloom was contagious. She moved her hands this way and that. Give him her full face, profile, *profile perdu*. Nothing pleased him. In less than an hour Rosalie stepped down from the stand, announcing that she was through for the day. And for any day, she added to herself as she faced Algy's easel. Never again so long as she lived would she let herself in for anything so futile as having her portrait painted. Unless, of course, John Greenough – John Greehough indeed! A lousy promise breaker if ever there was one!

But the bitterest hate could never hold Rosalie for very long. By the time she reached the hotel anger had faded to resignation. Why not sit with Cousin Louisa for a while and let Miss Gryce go for a walk?

Miss Gryce was delighted. She wanted to visit her little patient at the Pueblo, but hadn't hoped to get off so soon.

In her grey-blue linen and white hat Miss Gryce looked very handsome as she passed through the hall. Where should she go to buy a present for little Peter? What would he like most? The toys at the curio shop wouldn't appeal to him. Perhaps he would like a knife. A new clean knife was safer than a rusty one.

She stepped into the grocery store, large and dark, smelling of tar and molasses. At length she decided on a small hunting knife with a leather sheath and a loop to hang it from one's belt.

She was turning off the high road into the lane that led to the Pueblo, when a voice from the hedge said, "Good morning!" and Professor Bridges stepped down into the road. Miss Gryce was pleased. When she said she was on her way to the Pueblo the professor asked if he might accompany her, and she agreed with alacrity.

He carried a long, cylindrical, green tin case on a strap slung over one shoulder; a vasculum, he explained, for the transportation of any interesting botanical specimens that he might find during his explorations of the countryside.

The Pueblo was not accustomed to the arrival of visitors on foot. For a moment, as on the day before, the scene was brilliantly alive with colour and movement. Then laughter and talk died, women and children scuttled under cover. Leaving Professor Bridges to botanise beside the stream, Miss Gryce went on across the bridge.

Peter came running to meet her, followed more sedately by his father, James Rio. The three moved across the yard to James Rio's apartment. The cut was examined, found to be doing nicely, Peter was told that he might take off the bandage next day. Then she presented the knife. Dumb with gratitude, Peter hung it on his belt. James Rio smiled. They returned to where the professor sat at the edge of the stream examining a minute dripping sprig of green through a magnifying glass.

Miss Gryce suggested a stroll around the Pueblo. James Rio agreed with alacrity. "Our ruined church is very curious," he began, and broke off. A woman was beckoning to him from across the yard. He nodded and turned to Miss Gryce:

"A message from Wind-from-the-mountain, my grandfather," he explained.

"Wind-from-the-mountain, my grandfather, wishes to speak with the white woman who has been kind to Little Poplar Tree – Little Poplar Tree is the Indian name for my boy Peter. Wind-from-the-mountain, my grandfather, wishes to thank the white woman for her good deed." He hesitated. "Wind from the mountain is a great chief, but he is old. He is nearly a hundred years old. Miss Gryce knows that the old are not pleasant to look at? And not always kind in speech?"

Miss Gryce assured him that she was accustomed to making allowances for old people and would be delighted to meet a great chief. The professor said he too would like to pay his respects.

They all turned back and followed James Rio to the door where the woman stood waiting.

James Rio paused in the low doorway, bent his head and led the way into a very small low-ceilinged room, windowless and so dark that for a moment they could see nothing. Then, slowly, a figure in one corner took shape; a bundled-up figure, like a mummy set on end and propped up in a large wooden chair, with feet in sky-blue moccasins protruding at one end, and at the top, a slice of dark wizened face showing under a scarlet scarf bound tight around the temples. The eyes were shut, the jaws mumbled silently.

James Rio touched the bundle gently, bent close, and whispered. The eyes opened; filmy eyes, pupil and iris bleared to a general glassiness like grey agate. But the head nodded and the lips moved.

James Rio bent lower, listening deferentially. The old chief repeated his remark in a voice so suddenly loud and firm that everybody jumped. James Rio stood erect.

"Wind-from-the-Mountain, my grandfather, bids me tell the white woman that he thanks her for her good deed to Little Poplar Tree."

Janet Gryce nodded and smiled.

The old chief spoke again. James Rio interpreted: "Wind-from-the-Mountain, my grandfather, bids me tell the white woman that he will send her a present. A very nice present."

Miss Gryce tried to show her gratitude by more smiles and nods. But the old man's eyes were already shut again. Obviously the interview was at an end. They all tiptoed out of doors.

They walked on to the ruined church where Peter was waiting for them. One dark gaunt tower, left after bombardment by the United States Army, still held its own against wind and rain bent on reducing the adobe to its original clay. The walls lay strewn along the ground, making an irregular quadrangle that sheltered a few small white wooden crosses.

"The graves of the chiefs who were executed after the rebellion,"

James Rio explained. "And here," he pointed to a row of stones embedded in the earth in front of the ruins, "here is where the six trees grew which served as their gallows."

Janet Gryce shuddered. "Six of them? How sickening! It happened long long ago, I suppose?"

"The last rebellion of my people was eighty – ninety – years ago. But the trees died that same winter."

"Mortified at being asked to bear such dreadful fruit," Professor Bridges observed. James Rio nodded.

There was a moment's silence, then Miss Gryce remarked: "These stones are all dark red except one. Why is that one white?"

"It stands for the tree on which my great-grandfather, Desert Eagle, was hung," James Rio explained. "It is a white stone because my great-grandfather, Desert Eagle, was innocent. He knew that fighting the armies of the United States was like fighting the lightning. The day of the murder of Governor Dane he was far away from here at Acoma. But they hung him with the others."

Miss Gryce and the professor could only shake their heads sadly. They bade good-bye to the Rios, father and son, and returned to the hotel.

Miss Gryce arrived in time to help her employer dress. After a hearty lunch and a nap Mrs Kearny-Pine, leaning on Miss Gryce's arm, made her usual progress downstairs to the living room and afternoon tea.

As the clock struck five, Algy arrived. Aunt Louisa was hell on punctuality. Miss Gryce retired. Rosalie poured out the tea.

"So Uncle Steve is coming?" Algy remarked as he sipped his tea.

Mrs Kearny-Pine frowned. "Yes. He'll be here very soon. I'm almost sorry now that I sent for him. But I thought I was going to have a bad heart attack."

"Uncle Steve would want to be with you if you were really ill – which Heaven forbid! And you would want to have him."

"Well, as it turns out, I don't need him. I feel quite well this afternoon. However, it doesn't matter. Stephen can go right back East again."

7

In the next few days life at the hotel went on without special incident. To her great satisfaction, Rosalie was able to escape from Cousin Louisa for most of the day now. Mrs Kearny-Pine not only napped in the afternoon but had decided to breakfast in bed and very late in order to gather strength for the approaching arrival of her husband, which was sure to be fatiguing.

As usual in the latter part of the afternoon the hall was crowded. Professor Bridges had begun telling an interested audience of his adventures that morning when he was interrupted by the sound of a motor horn. Everybody looked toward the front door. Pedro sprang to open it. A massive figure strode in. "Mrs Kearny-Pine's husband!" everybody murmured to everybody else.

Stephen Pine gave Pedro a nod, a circular nod introducing Pedro to the car outside. Pedro dashed out for the luggage. Mr Pine glared around the hall, strode to the desk, angrily scrawled a signature, muttered, and strode upstairs in Pedro's wake without so much as glancing at anyone in the hall.

All eyes followed him. Nobody paid the slightest attention to a dowdy little clergyman who had slipped in with Pedro and the luggage.

He approached the desk, accepted the register clapped down in front of him by Mr Miller, and wrote a timid "Rev. S. Wurtz, Jakesville, Ohio," beneath Mr Pine's flamboyant signature.

In the meantime Mr Pine was striding along the upstairs corridor. Rosalie recognized his powerful tread and emerged from her room. He kissed her, but his kiss was absent and unenthusiastic.

"Which is Louisa's room?" he barked, banged at the door Rosalie indicated, and bounced in.

Miss Gryce looked out of her room next to that of Mrs

Kearny-Pine. Rosalie joined her. They both stood listening in astonishment to the roarings and bellowings of Mr Pine's voice. Every word he said could be distinctly heard through the thin partition, and Mrs Kearny-Pine's answers could be guessed at.

"Do you mean to tell me, Louisa, that you brought me all the way from New York to this godforsaken hole just to tell me that Marie was dead and you had a bad dream? Dreams be damned. Indigestion. Too much of that damned afternoon tea of yours and a damn sight too many muffins. You're always jawing me about cocktails. Louisa, will you get down to brass tacks and tell me why you sent for me? Well, if you won't, you won't. Talk about a mule's hind legs. Are you through? Then I have something to say, Louisa. I want a divorce and I want it quick. Well, that's a detail. We'll go into all that tomorrow before I leave. Of course I'm leaving. Do I want to look at tepees and sit in wigwams? We'll go into all that tomorrow, I tell you! Which is my room? I want to change before dinner."

A door banged. There was a moment's silence. Rosalie giggled. "He's a bull in a china shop, isn't he? A raving mad bull too."

But Miss Gryce listened with anxiety. "Excitement isn't good for her," she remarked. "You know, Mrs Kearny-Pine really has a bad murmur. I'd like to give her some ammonia."

The bellowing suddenly broke out again: "Why should I have a filthy little room over the kitchen just because it's next to yours? What are you afraid of, anyway? Isn't a big husky trained nurse protection enough? All right. But I will not keep the door open in between. And I warn you, Louisa, if I catch so much as one snore from you I'll come in and shoot your head off."

Rosalie hadn't looked forward to dinner, but it wasn't, after all, as uncomfortable as she had expected. Alvarez the chef had laid himself out to please the distinguished guest from New York, and he had succeeded. If Mrs Kearny-Pine was uneasy she kept it to herself. Rosalie's frock was charming and she chattered along about nothing in the way Stephen Pine liked girls to do. As he sipped his coffee, very good coffee, he found his mood softening. The tennis courts you saw through the dining room window looked fairly decent, and if Rosalie was right about that Harvard man's game it mightn't be a bad idea to stop over a day or two.

And when they returned to the hall after dinner, such was the amelioration of Mr Pine's condition that, finding his late travelling companion at his elbow, he introduced the little clergyman to his wife and to Rosalie. Mrs Kearny-Pine gave the little parson a frosty smile and indicated a chair at her side. He sat down timidly. But she was accustomed to shy clergymen and at once began putting him at his ease.

In a few minutes she knew all about his parish in Ohio and the difficulties with the choir that had caused a nervous breakdown. But her tactful pumping brought a scanter flow than she usually drew forth. She suppressed a yawn, and when the little man ventured to suggest that the hour was late, she was more than willing to let him go.

Nevertheless, when Stephen Pine betook himself to bed, he was in an uncomfortable frame of mind. It was all very well to pretend that he was staying on in Tecos because of good tennis courts and a horse race at the Pueblo. In point of fact, he was staying on with the hope of persuading Louisa to change her mind about a divorce, and that was a very faint hope indeed. His conversation with Louisa on the subject had been badly bungled. Would he never learn that Louisa's obstinacy was the obstinacy of a baulky mule and that in a contest of wills she always came out on top? Yes, it was going to take a lot of handling to make Louisa see things his way, Steve decided, as he kicked off his shoes. God alone knew how long it might be before he was able to leave for Santa Barbara – Santa Barbara and Arabella.

8

In the hall the clerk, Mr Miller, was sorting the morning mail. Miss Gryce was standing beside the desk waiting for the letters, when a little Indian boy appeared at the front door and peeped shyly in. She smiled, recognizing Peter from the Pueblo, and he advanced to the desk and held out a package.

"For me?" Miss Gryce exclaimed, as she took it and, unfolding a scrap of newspaper, drew out a pair of turquoise blue doeskin moccasins soft as silk and intricately beaded. "How perfectly lovely!"

"It is a gift from Wind-from-the-Mountain, my grandfather," Peter said breathlessly – evidently he had learned the sentence by heart – and, smiling with relief at having accomplished his mission, he ran off to the kitchen.

Rosalie came strolling across the room, admired the moccasins, and turned to the clerk. "Any letters for me, Mr Miller?" she asked. She looked slightly annoyed, for Miss Gryce had already gathered up the pile of letters for Mrs Kearny-Pine's family and was walking off with them to the living room. As she went, Miss Gryce sorted them, and slipped two into her wrist bag before she gave the remainder to her employer, who took them with a reproving frown.

"You need not sort the mail, Miss Gryce," she said stiffly. "I prefer to look over the letters myself before they are distributed."

"Sorry," Miss Gryce bit her lip. "I'll remember another time, Mrs Kearny-Pine," and she walked upstairs.

Mrs Kearny-Pine glanced at the letters in her hand, examining each envelope before she handed them one by one to Rosalie and to her husband, who had followed Miss Gryce and the mail and now stood waiting impatiently.

"Here are your letters, Stephen," she said, adding a careless:

"Who is writing to you from Santa Barbara?" which brought no answer.

Stephen moved away and stood with his back turned to his wife as he opened his letters. "Nothing of any interest for me," she went on.

"I certainly ought to have heard from the 'Infant Paupers' by now. Two letters for you, Rosalie. What does your Aunt Mary say?"

Rosalie tore open the two envelopes, glanced at them indifferently. "Aunt Mary wants me to buy her a turquoise bracelet," she said, "and the other is only an advertisement. Not worth waiting for. Cousin Steve, are you ready? You know we were going to play tennis at Miss Joy's."

But Cousin Steve did not seem to hear her. He stood kicking the burning logs in the fireplace with the toe of his shoe; which gave off a horrible smell of scorched rubber.

"Cousin Steve," she said again. "Aren't you coming?"

He turned, glared at her, muttered "No tennis today. Better go without me," and stamped off to the writing room back of the hall.

Rosalie looked after him in surprise. Why was Cousin Steve's face so red? And he had a queer glittery look in his eyes. She glanced at Cousin Louisa. But apparently that lady had not observed her husband's abrupt departure. She was absorbed in reading a letter written on bright pink paper, holding it at arm's length as if it had an unpleasant smell. Rosalie was turning away when Mrs Kearny-Pine called her back.

"Rosalie," she snapped, so sharply that Rosalie jumped. Something queer about Cousin Louisa too, she looked as mad as a hornet. "Rosalie, I want you to leave a note at Algy's studio." She took a pencil and a scrap of paper from her work bag, scribbled a hasty line and folded the paper into a cocked hat. "Get me a telegraph blank and an envelope from the desk."

Rosalie brought them. Mrs Kearny-Pine wrote a message, put it into the envelope, licked the flap with indignant decision and handed both missives to Rosalie.

"There!" she snorted. "Send the telegram, and leave the note at Algy's studio on your way to Miss Joy's. No answer," she added grimly. And Rosalie departed.

Mrs Kearny-Pine resumed her embroidery, jabbing her needle through her needlepoint as if she were impaling a noxious insect with every stitch. Now and then she emitted a gurgle of anger, or muttered a name under her breath "Myrtle Cream, indeed! *Myrtle Cream!*"

But there was no one to hear these angry sounds. She was free to indulge her emotions unobserved. At this hour the hall was deserted. As soon as the morning mail had been distributed the guests had, as usual, dispersed. Miss Gryce was in her room, writing more postal cards. The servants were having their dinner, all except Lost Arrow, who sat on the sidewalk playing jack stones. Mr Miller had an hour off at this time of day and spent it taking a nap in his bedroom.

As for Stephen Pine, he was sitting alone in the writing room too far off to hear his wife's indignant exclamations. Nor would he have cared if he had heard. He was much too absorbed in his own correspondence, a letter which he read over and over, groaning and running his fingers wildly through his hair until every hair stood on end.

Mrs Kearny-Pine glanced at the clock. Not quite time yet for her morning glass of milk. She had half a mind not to wait for it. She might visit the curio shop, and tell Mr Crowder the result of her inquiries about the Blue Santo. But she wasn't sure she felt well enough to go by herself. Rosalie should have stayed with her. Rosalie oughtn't to go rummaging all over the place, paying so little attention. Rosalie was very inconsiderate.

At lunch time the hall began filling up again. In the dining room the tables were already set when Rosalie returned. Cousin Louisa wasn't in the hall or in the living room. Rosalie went on upstairs to have a bath before lunch.

She came down again half an hour later, expecting to get the usual scolding for unpunctuality from Cousin Louisa. But Cousin Louisa hadn't yet come down. Rosalie waited a few minutes, went upstairs, knocked at Cousin Louisa's door. There was no answer.

Miss Gryce's door opened and Miss Gryce looked out. Her face was pale and there were dark circles under her eyes.

"Isn't Cousin Louisa coming down to lunch?" Rosalie asked. "Doesn't she feel well?"

"Mrs Kearny-Pine is downstairs," Miss Gryce said. "At least I left her there with her embroidery some time ago and I haven't heard her return to her room."

Rosalie opened the door of Mrs Kearny-Pine's room. "She isn't here," she remarked. "But I didn't see her downstairs, and I looked everywhere. Except in the writing room. Perhaps she's there with Cousin Steve."

But Cousin Louisa wasn't in the writing room. Cousin Steve said he hadn't seen her all the morning. He looked positively haggard now, Rosalie said to herself. And he muttered and waved his hands with such a sort of crazy look, when Rosalie kept on wondering where Cousin Louisa could have gone to at this time of day, that she felt quite frightened.

"How should I know where Louisa is!" he growled. "Can't you see I'm busy?" The floor was strewn with torn scraps of paper, and the blotter on the desk where he sat, laid fresh by Pedro that morning, was splotched with ink. "No, I don't want any lunch. For God's sake, Rosalie will you clear out!"

Rosalie, wondering, turned towards the dining room, and paused. Cousin Louisa must have gone out for a walk. But Cousin Louisa didn't like to go out alone because of her weak heart. She ran upstairs again and met Miss Gryce coming down, looking worried.

"Has Mrs Kearny-Pine returned?" the latter asked.

"Returned?" Rosalie exclaimed. "Did she go out then?"

"She must have. Her grey coat and hat and her lilac parasol

are not on the bed where she told me to lay them this morning. Perhaps she went to the curio shop."

"That's it, of course." Rosalie looked relieved. "She must have come up and got her things and gone down again. But I should think you would have heard her, Miss Gryce."

Miss Gryce reflected. "No; I wouldn't have heard her. I've been typing postals all the morning, and it's a noisy machine."

"Well, I suppose she'll soon be back," Rosalie said uncertainly. "We'd better have lunch."

They went down to the hall. "I'll wait here for her." Miss Gryce said. "She'll be tired and hot when she comes in. She may want me."

Rosalie glanced at the clock. "After two!" she exclaimed. "Don't you think it's very strange for Cousin Louisa to go out all by herself and not come back in time for lunch? She's so frightfully punctual as a rule."

"It is strange," Miss Gryce admitted.

"Could the walk and the heat have been too much for her? Perhaps she had to stop somewhere to rest."

"Perhaps." Miss Gryce looked still more worried. "I do hope she hasn't had a heart attack."

"Oh, poor Cousin Louisa!" Rosalie cried. "I'm afraid that's exactly what has happened. I'll run and tell Cousin Steve. And make him pay attention, no matter how busy he is."

She hurried to the writing room. "Cousin Steve, I'm sorry to disturb you, but Miss Gryce and I are worried about Cousin Louisa. It seems she went out for a walk a little while ago and she hasn't come back. It's long past lunch time, and Miss Gryce is afraid she's had a heart attack. In the street, perhaps!"

"What's that?" Steve drew his hand across his eyes and spoke thickly. "What's that? Louisa is late for lunch?"

"We are afraid she has been taken ill," Rosalie insisted. "Do rouse yourself, Cousin Steve. Come out in the hall and speak to Mr Miller. He may be able to suggest something. He might send

Pedro to the curio shop."

But Steve had slumped down again into his chair. "Do whatever you like, Rosalie," he murmured and resumed his writing.

Rosalie looked at him in despair and returned to Miss Gryce.

"Cousin Steve refuses to take the slightest interest," she said impatiently. "He doesn't seem to care one bit whether poor Cousin Louisa dies in the street or not! What had we better do, Miss Gryce?"

"Someone must have seen her go out," Miss Gryce suggested, "and they might have noticed which direction she went."

"Of course, Mr Miller would have seen her, or Pedro – he's always lounging on the sidewalk."

But the clerk said he had not happened to see Mrs Kearny-Pine starting out for her walk. As usual, he had left the desk after the mail had been sorted. When he returned a little after twelve she had already gone out. There was nobody in the hall except Mr Atwater, who said he was waiting for his aunt, and the clerk had suggested phoning up to her room, but Mr Atwater had said it didn't matter, and had hung around for a few minutes, as if he didn't know what to do, and then hurried away.

"Upset, he seemed," the clerk commented. "Kind of worried. Went off at a dead run down the street. Mr Atwater don't move so awful quick as a rule."

Pedro was summoned from the kitchen. But neither had Pedro happened to see Mrs Kearny-Pine starting out. It seemed that Pedro had been absent for quite a while between eleven and twelve o'clock. Mr Pine had sent him to the telegraph office with a message Mr Pine said was too long to send over the phone. It was in a sealed envelope but the operator had read it over half aloud to make sure he understood it.

Pedro obligingly began repeating the telegram but had only got as far as "Mrs A. Larkin, Santa Barbara," when the clerk, with a sidelong glance at Rosalie, stopped him.

And Lost Arrow, when he was appealed to, also declared that

he had seen nothing of Mrs Kearny-Pine. But he acknowledged, after close questioning from Mr Miller and Pedro, that he had left his post for a few minutes during the hour in question to have a soda in the drug store with a friend.

Pedro then suggested that Bella might have seen her. Bella was a bright girl and observant. She might have been in the dining room when Mrs Kearny-Pine passed through the hall and noticed which way the lady turned after reaching the street. This seemed promising. But it was found that, unluckily, Bella had left the hotel and gone home, as it was her afternoon off, and the other waitresses had been too busy setting their tables for lunch to notice anything else.

"We're wasting time," Rosalie exclaimed. "Pedro, I want you to go around to the curio shop and ask Mr Crowder if Mrs Kearny-Pine has been there this morning. I'll go to Mr Atwater's studio myself. He hasn't a telephone."

"I suppose I'd best stay here in case Mrs Kearny-Pine is feeling ill when she comes back?" Miss Gryce put in.

Rosalie nodded and hurried away.

But nobody answered her rat-tat-tat on Algy's door. She fancied she could hear someone moving about inside, and she banged the knocker up and down impatiently, but nobody came. She turned the knob but the door was locked. At length, hot and anxious now, Rosalie ran back to the hotel, telling herself that of course Cousin Louisa would in the meantime have returned, very cross at hearing of all this fuss about nothing.

But Cousin Louisa had not yet returned. Guests were coming out from lunch, standing around and talking in the hall.

John Greenough came forward. "I hear you are worried about your aunt," he said. "Is there anything I can do? Anywhere you'd like me to go?"

"I don't know," Rosalie hesitated. "Cousin Steve ought to be here. I wish you'd speak to him – he's in the writing room. Try to make him understand that Miss Gryce and I are really worried about Cousin Louisa. I tried, but he didn't seem to care one bit."

She broke off. "Here's Pedro. Pedro, what did Mr Crowder say? Had she been to the curio shop?"

Mr Crowder says that Mrs Kearny-Pine has not been to the curio shop today," Pedro answered solemnly. "And I have spoken to several people who might have seen her when she started off for her walk, but no one did. Where do you want me to go next, Miss Colbrook?"

"Can you suggest anything, Miss Gryce?" Rosalie asked distractedly, and then: "Here is Cousin Steve at last!"

For Greenough's appeal had been successful. He and Steve returned together, and the latter seemed now to realize the seriousness of the situation.

He looked exceedingly anxious, and when his attention was called to the hour – after three o'clock – he took a gloomy view. Undoubtedly his poor wife had had a heart attack and been carried into someone's house, perhaps in a dying condition. He shuddered. Perhaps she was already dead.

"My poor Louisa," he groaned. "My poor, poor Louisa!"

Rosalie stamped her foot. "Don't go on like that, Cousin Steve. What's the use? We've got to find where she went."

Steve only nodded vaguely. John Greenough interposed:

"You might take a car, Mr Pine, and visit all the studios beyond the represa, while you and I, Rosalie, go to the ones on this side. I would also suggest sending Pedro to the Pueblo. There isn't one chance in a thousand that Mrs Kearny-Pine got as far as the Pueblo, but someone there might have seen her this morning and Pedro will get information from the locals more easily than we could. And Mr Miller might call up the druggist and Mr Garcia's store, and anybody else in Tecos who has a telephone, and ask if they have seen her go by."

Mr Greenough's advice seemed good and was taken. Everybody did exactly what he told them to.

An hour went by. Miss Gryce still sat in the hall waiting, her face drawn now with lines of anxiety. It was a little after four when Mr Pine returned. Miss Gryce sprang to her feet and hurried to the door to meet him. He sank down on a chair, mopping his face.

"I've been to every place I could think of," he groaned. "When Louisa walked out of here she seems to have vanished as completely as if she'd stepped into a manhole in the sidewalk. Most extraordinary. Has Rosalie got back yet?"

"Here she comes now," Miss Gryce exclaimed. "I do hope she has heard something."

But Rosalie and John Greenough had been as unsuccessful as Mr Pine. They had gone first to Mr Magilp's studio and then to Miss Joy's, as being the most likely places for Mrs Kearny-Pine to have visited, but she had not been seen there, and they had tried the other studios in Tecos without result. They had gone to Algy's studio again on the chance that he was back, but the door was still locked. And they had ended by knocking at every single door of every adobe, little and big, this side of the represa. But no one had caught even a glimpse of any lady answering to the description of Mrs Kearny-Pine.

Stephen Pine, Rosalie, John Greenough and Miss Gryce were standing looking at each other in deep perplexity, while the clerk and Pedro hovered uncertainly in the background, surrounded by a penumbra of whispering guests, when Mrs Couch suddenly appeared on the scene.

Mrs Couch had been away all day on a trip to a distant ranch and was terribly disturbed when she was told that Mrs Kearny-Pine, known to be subject to heart attacks, had gone for a walk shortly before lunch and never come back. She grasped at once the seriousness of the situation – not only for the bereaved family, but for her hotel – and showed her usual business ability without a moment's delay. Messengers, on foot and on horseback, were despatched in many directions, with orders given by Mrs Couch and enforced by threats and arguments and bribes that she had found effectual on previous occasions when information she happened to want was not forthcoming.

But nothing whatever resulted from Mrs Couch's energetic and experienced methods. Night fell. It was useless to go on searching in the dark. John Greenough said sternly that if Rosalie wouldn't be sensible and get some rest, he most certainly would not take her chasing all over the country next day, and, at last, very unwillingly, she went to her room.

Miss Gryce followed. As Rosalie departed, a strangled "I'm all in!" burst from the nurse, and she ran sobbing upstairs. In a few minutes everybody else had dragged themselves off and gone to bed, determined to get a little sleep out of what was left of the night.

9

Rosalie woke with a start to find that dawn had come. She dressed hurriedly. Pedro was bringing in breakfast – hot coffee, a huge dish of bacon and eggs – when she reached the dining room. But neither she nor any member of the anxious family group could take the smallest interest in food. In less than ten minutes everybody pushed back their chairs and expressed themselves ready to start out.

Some twenty men were waiting on the sidewalk for instructions. Unfortunately, one important field of inquiry had to be abandoned for the time being. The Pueblo could not be searched for a reason that even Mrs Couch found herself unable to ignore. The old chief was dead.

He had died very suddenly. The Pueblo was buzzing like a hive and would continue to buzz until after the funeral. Anyhow, searching the Pueblo was a matter of form. No one really supposed that Mrs Kearny-Pine with her weak heart could have walked as far as the Pueblo, and it would have been known at the garage if she had driven there.

As the sun rose, the street began to fill with spectators. It was a lively scene. Jonas Train – Mr Magilp's model for his cowboy pictures – rode a spirited horse that went bucking back and forth across the street.

The searchers were all mounted. For it had been decided that Mrs Kearny-Pine must have departed in some sort of vehicle, or she would have been found by now, as every place within walking distance had been already examined. Perhaps a friend had met her in the street and asked her to go for a drive? Perhaps this friend had driven her to some distant ranch and invited her to spend the night?

"But Cousin Louisa hasn't any friends out here," Rosalie broke in, as these various suggestions were offered by one person and another. "And she wouldn't dream of spending the night anywhere without sending for Miss Gryce, because of her weak heart. I've said again and again that the only suspicious place is Governor Dane's house, that horrid little adobe where Cousin Louisa got such a fright the other day. I know – don't ask me how – l know that Cousin Louisa's disappearance is in some way connected with that house!"

"But I tell you I went there," Steve put in fretfully. "And the woman swore Louisa hadn't set foot in the house except that one time."

"Well, I'm going to see for myself," Rosalie persisted. "Do the men all know what they are to do, Mrs Couch?"

"They understand that they'll be well paid for their time?" Steve put in. "Tell them I'll make the everlasting fortune of any man who finds my wife, or brings us the smallest clue to go on."

"I've told them that," Mrs Couch answered, "and they're just crazy to be off."

She waved her hand. There was a shout, a whistle of quirts, clatter of horses' hoofs, a great jingling of harness, and the slap of bare feet padding along the sidewalk. A cloud of dust and the road was empty.

"And now we can start off ourselves," Rosalie remarked. "You are going to that dude ranch at Alcalde, aren't you, Cousin Steve? It's a long drive, but I suppose you'll be back by dinner time?"

Steve Pine nodded without speaking, and was turning away when Greenough ventured a suggestion "Don't you think Mrs Kearny-Pine's business manager, or her lawyer, would want to know that you are, temporarily, out of touch with her? Let me attend to it for you."

"All right. The address is Carboy and Patterson, 60 Wall Street – a bunch of old dodos – but wire them if you think best." He left them, walking heavily and muttering to himself.

"Cousin Steve seems all gone to pieces," Rosalie remarked to John Greenough. They were alone, Mrs Couch and Miss Gryce having gone indoors. "And somehow I'm just a little surprised. I never thought he and Cousin Louisa hit it off any too well. Another thing, did you notice that queer sort of frightened look in his eyes? He's worried, of course, but why should he look frightened?"

"You're letting your imagination run away with you," Greenough smiled. "But I agree that his nerves are in very bad shape. That's why I insisted on notifying Mrs Kearrny-Pine's lawyer, I'll get that telegram off as soon as the office is open. In the meantime, what about searching the murder house, Rosalie? Do you still want to go there?"

"I don't want to. I hate that little hole. But it's got to be done. Come along."

In that early morning light the plaza looked strangely unlike its daytime self. Rosalie and John Greenough walked through a narrow mud walled lane and reached the murder house. It showed no sign of life, the shutters were barred and the door closed. John Greenough rapped on the door with his stick. There was a long interval.

Eventually, a bolt was withdrawn, a key grated. The door opened on a crack and revealed a thin slice of face.

Everything was just the same today. The same smell, the same caretaker beckoning with the same skinny forefinger. John Greenough spoke to her in Spanish. She gave him a toothless smile. They stepped in. They were in a narrow passage lighted only by a single pane of glass set in a door at the rear. The woman pointed to the visitors' book on a stand, pen and inkwell beside it. A fly speckled placard hung above it.

While Rosalie signed their names in the book, John Greenough read:

"In this House Governor Dane was Foully Slain during the Indian Rebellion of 1848. His Murderers paid with their Lives. The full penalty for their Atrocious Crime."

Rosalie had turned back a page of the register. She motioned to Greenough. "Look," she whispered, "Cousin Louisa's signature! So shaky and blotted you can scarcely read it. She must have been frightened even then." She closed the book with a sigh. "Tell the woman we want to go all over the house from garret to cellar. Everywhere."

John Greenough explained, in Spanish, but the woman demurred. She had her orders. It was not permitted to show any but the two rooms open to the public, the room where the Governor had been murdered and his bedroom. She opened the door at the right of the entry and they went in.

The Governor had not lived luxuriously. The room was some ten feet square, and so low that even Rosalie could not stand upright. There was no furniture.

The caretaker unbarred the shutters and motioned to a dark blotch on the floor, murmuring a parrot-like recitation that Greenough did not trouble to translate. Rosalie turned away abruptly.

The other room was a twin of the first, except that the floor was not blood-stained. In the passage again, Rosalie said: "Ask her if Cousin Louisa has been here since that first day."

At this question, repeated in Spanish, the woman became voluble. "She says," he translated, "that the lady has not been here except that one time. She says she, Maria Vaca, remembers the lady because the lady gave her fifty cents and often the tourists give no more than ten cents and sometimes nothing."

John Greenough cut short these irrelevancies and brought the woman back to the point. "She says the lady signed the register," he went on, "and then entered the murder room. She unbarred the shutters and showed the lady the bloodstains – the bloodstains are what everybody desires to see first. Then, all of a sudden, the lady gave a cry and became very pale as if overcome by a sudden sickness. She had offered to bring a glass of water. But the lady had said 'No! No! No, just like that. No, No! No!' and pushed past her and out into the passage, and began fumbling at the door knob. And she, Maria Vaca, had opened the door at once, at once! And the lady had cried out to the young lady waiting for her outside. Yes, this same young lady who was here now."

"Ask her about the men that Cousin Louisa heard whispering in the back of the passage," Rosalie said.

The woman stared as Greenough put the question. She did not remember any whispering. Her husband might have been talking to his brother Jose. Unfortunately neither her husband nor his brother was at home. They had gone to Bernardino to buy a goat.

"Well, tell her I want to be shown all over the house," Rosalie insisted. "Not only the part that is open to the public, but the back yard and the garret and the cellar – everywhere."

Greenough repeated. The woman shook her head. That was not allowed. But Greenough pressed a five-dollar bill into her hand and she became suddenly affable.

If the young lady really wished to see the whole of this poor house, it would be a pleasure to show it to her. But the lady would be disappointed, there was little to see. No garret and no cellar. This was the way into the back yard. She unlocked the door in the rear wall.

It opened on a hard trodden space of yellow clay, mud walled, and empty except for a budding peach tree in one corner and a heap of garbage where two hens scratched disconsolately. The caretaker led the way across the yard and opened the door of a lean to stuck on to the main house like a mud dauber's nest. Rosalie forced herself to look in. It was the dirtiest and most forlorn human habitation she had ever seen.

Rosalie reluctantly expressed herself satisfied, and they returned to the house. As they went into the passage, Rosalie looked up. "There is a scuttle in the ceiling," she remarked. "Ask her where it leads to. She said there wasn't any garret."

But the woman only shook her head. Greenough got up on the stand to investigate.

"Nothing there," he said, coughing, "except dust and cobwebs. Just an empty hole."

He replaced the stand. They both thanked the woman. She opened the front door, bowing and smiling, and they went away.

"We couldn't have done anything more," Rosalie sighed. "But I still have a feeling that woman knows something. I wish I had told her to send her husband around to the hotel when he comes home. We might get more out of him, perhaps…"

"That can wait. Let's go back to the hotel now. You're as white as a sheet."

"I'm not tired," she protested. "Just jittery. It's the atmosphere of this place. Those Penitentes, you know, so cruel. Creeping about up there on the Mountain like in that awful picture of Algy's. And I've been wondering whether they – they could have got hold of poor Cousin Louisa – caught her spying on them and…"

"My dear girl, that's utter nonsense and you know it! How would she get up there on the Mountain? You're crazy! Plumb loony!"

"I suppose so." She smiled in spite of herself. "Anyway, don't let's go back to the hotel just yet. It's too early. There goes the Angelus now! What shall we do next, John?"

He saw she was too restless for inactivity. "Think back," he said. "Can you recall any recent occurrence, no matter how trivial – besides Mrs Kearny-Pine's visit to the murder house – that seemed in any way suspicious, or unusual?"

She paused, murmured a doubtful: "What else did we do that day?" Then, with rising excitement: "I remember now, we went to Mr Crowder's curio shop to look for a Blue Santo and a rough looking man came in while we were there – and Cousin Louisa was wearing her pearls – and Mr Crowder admired them and said they were very valuable and the man might have been listening and perhaps he was a thief and if he did turn out to be a thief, that would be a clue, John! A real clue! Don't you think that would be a clue?"

"It might be. Anyway, we'll go and have a talk with Mr Crowder."

The town had begun to wake up now, and although the curio shop was still closed when Rosalie and John Greenough arrived there, Mr Crowder saw them from an upper window, came hurrying down and ushered them in without a moment's delay.

He couldn't at first recall any rough looking man having entered the shop during Mrs Kearny-Pine's recent visit. Then it came to him, a man from Iowa had wanted to buy a toy. The curio toys weren't cheap enough and he had been told to try at Garcia's. As Mr Crowder remembered him, he was a decent looking fellow. Fording it West with his family, intending to spend the night in the motor camp on the Eagle Peak Road.

Five minutes walk brought them to the motor camp. A dozen flimsy shacks, painted red, facing a strip of bare, sun baked earth. Only one showed signs of life, for summer travel had not yet begun. Here a Model T stood against the wall. On the doorstep a man sat crouched with a baby in his arms, feeding it from a bottle, smoke rose from a fire built on the ground and tended by a pretty little boy.

As Rosalie and Greenough approached, the man looked up inquiringly. He had a gaunt weather beaten face, set with china blue eyes. Rosalie recognized him, it was the man she had seen in the curio shop. He stirred, the bottle was withdrawn, and the little creature in his arms let out a wail of anger.

"Poor darling," Rosalie murmured, bending over the baby as the man hurriedly rammed the nipple back into the wide open toothless mouth. "It's awfully hungry, isn't it?"

"He's always hungry," the man said resignedly. "Some way, there don't seem to be no plumb to this child. And milk ain't easy come by when you're on the road. Now Buddie here – with a proud glance at the little boy – he chaws bacon and beans like I do."

"You are taking care of the children all by yourself?" Rosalie exclaimed.

"Yes ma'am. My wife, she up and died five weeks ago. So I sold out and we're moving West."

"How did you happen to come to Tecos?" John Greenough put in. "It's a long way off the main road."

"It sure is. But my wife's sister, she lives here and I hoped she'd keep Josiah – that's the baby – till I got my bearings. But she's sick and I've been waiting round while she made up her mind. Now she says she ain't well enough. So we're pushing on soon's the kids have had their breakfast."

Rosalie kissed the children, and was turning to go, when Greenough paused. "Where does that trail lead to?" he asked the man, indicating a path that mounted up the hill behind the camp. "Isn't it one of the trails to Eagle Peak?"

"I wouldn't know," the man answered. "But my wife's sister, she said I'd do well to keep Buddie close to camp. Seems they's mighty queer doings up and down them paths round Easter time."

"Penitentes?" Rosalie breathed, but Greenough shook his head.

"I know that cliff well," he said, "and there isn't a single Penitente calvary anywhere on it."

"I seen a man went up," Buddie put in solemnly. "And he didn't never come back."

"Must have been yesterday," his father remarked, "whilst I was at the store."

"Did he look like an Indian, or a Mexican, Buddie?" Rosalie asked.

But the child only stared. She went on, "Was he wearing a coat, a nice coat like Mr Greenough's?" Buddie nodded. "An American then," Greenough said. "Ten to one it was Magilp. Would you like a climb, Rosalie? I want to get a painting stool I left up there the other day. Or shall we go back to the hotel now?" She hesitated, and he went on "It will be hours before any news comes in…"

"Hours of just sitting around and waiting," she sighed. "And I've always wanted to climb Eagle Peak. Let's go!"

Ten minutes' steady climb brought them, with dazzling suddenness, out of dark, moist, cool forest shadow into hot, dry, windy sunlight.

Shading their eyes, they stepped out onto a ledge of rock, carpeted with dry turf, overlooking a vast expanse, of plain and mountain shimmering in a haze of blue and violet and pale gold far below.

"I thought this was where you came to paint your bird's eye view of the Pueblo," Rosalie remarked in some surprise, as she stood staring out over the rim of the cliff down into the abyss and across the plain. "But I don't see it anywhere."

"You can't see it from here. My painting place is farther down. Beyond that boulder," he said, pointing. "Better take my hand. The rocks are rough and apt to crumble. One misstep would be our last!"

They moved slowly and carefully down the cliff side. As they rounded the boulder and came in sight of another ledge overhung by a wind twisted pine tree. Greenough exclaimed: "Why, there's my stool! I thought I had put it under a bush and it's right out on the edge where I've been painting. I wonder it didn't blow away."

"Rather careless of you," Rosalie observed, as they stepped out on the ledge. "I still don't get your view of the Pueblo," she went on, drawing her hand from his to shade her eyes

"The tree comes in between. You have to get a bit lower, so you can see under the branches. Sit down on my stool." He took her hand again. "Now look…. Oh my God!"

She was screaming, high and shrill, wild with terror, toppling forward – falling – falling – falling out – over – dragging on his hand. But his fingers had caught her wrist in a fierce grip. Grinding his heels into the turf, pitting his weight against hers, he braced himself, flung himself backward. For one agonizing second she seemed to dangle in space. Then a final gasping, straining effort jerked her to safety. Together they fell sprawling full length on the turf and lay there panting.

He was on his feet at once. She lay still, white and shivering; then drew a long breath and sat up, her hands clasping her knees.

They stared dizzily at each other.

"God!" he muttered, his face as white as hers. "That was a narrow shave!"

"What – what happened?"

"The damn stool broke under you. It's gone. Gone over." He moved forward.

She caught him back with a shuddering: "Don't-don't go to the edge! I can't bear it!"

"I'll be careful." He dropped to his hands and knees, and crawled to the rim.

"It's there," he said. "In pieces, of course. The screw must have fetched loose – it's a tripod, held together with a screw. But I'll swear it was all right the last time I used it. Oh well, no use guessing."

Retreating from the edge of the precipice, he dropped on the turf beside her and surveyed her small pale face with anxious concern. She clasped her trembling knees still tighter and managed a smile.

"God forgive me," he sighed. "I'll never forgive myself. Careless fool. I should never have brought you up here. Suppose you had been killed. How could I have borne to go on living!"

"No need to worry about *that*," she said. "If I had gone over, you would have gone too, you know. Anyway, neither of us is dead. We're both alive!" She laughed and sprang to her feet. "We're alive and the sun is shining and it's a beautiful world and I'm so hungry I could eat a house. Come on! Let's go! Breakfast time, John, let's go! I don't mind going back to the hotel now. I have a hunch we'll find Cousin Louisa there in the dining room, enjoying her breakfast, but cross as two sticks and ready to bite our heads off because of all the fuss."

10

Rosalie's hopes were not justified. The hotel proved as barren of news as when they had left it. The hired searchers were still searching. Stephen Pine had sent no reassuring message from Alcalde.

Rosalie and John Greenough were still at table when the Santa Fe newspapers began making themselves annoying over the telephone. Mrs Couch did her best. She answered the calls herself and, having no regard whatever for inconvenient facts, was able to ward off inquiry for the time being. But she knew the respite would be brief and laid down the receiver with a sigh of exasperation. Another hour brought calls from all over the county, and she was soon obliged to admit defeat.

The morning wore away. An anxious telegram came from Carboy and Patterson demanding information but giving none. Just before lunch Miss Joy and Mr Magilp came in to offer their services and make suggestions. Rosalie joined them in the hall, followed by Greenough and Professor Bridges.

Mr Magilp thought it would be well to explore some of the canyons in the vicinity, and offered to do so. Professor Bridges mentioned several almost inaccessible trails that might be overlooked by persons less familiar with the country than himself.

"Trails! Canyons!" Rosalie exclaimed. "Why, you forget you're talking of Cousin Louisa. Cousin Louisa couldn't climb anywhere – couldn't even take a long walk. You don't mean. You don't think?" She faltered – stopped, looking from one serious face to another.

They avoided her anxious eyes. No one spoke for a moment. Then Magilp said solemnly:

"We must face facts, Miss Colbrook, no matter how painful they may be. As Mrs Kearny-Pine has neither returned home nor sent any message to her family, we are forced to the conclusion that something more serious must have occurred to delay her than a fainting spell resulting from too long a walk, or an unexpected visit to a friend." He hesitated, went on reluctantly, "Do you consider Mrs Kearny-Pine a morbid person? Have you noticed any symptoms of nervous strain recently?"

Rosalie stared, bewildered. "Why, no. Cousin Louisa was a very calm person. I never saw her really excited about anything. As for being morbid, I don't quite see..." She broke off shuddering. "If you mean suicide, that's absolutely out of the question – the very last thing Cousin Louisa would ever have thought of. She always said suicide was both wicked and silly."

"Just so," Magilp nodded. "Well then, Miss Colbrook, I fear – I greatly fear – that Mrs Kearny-Pine has met with foul play."

"Foul play!" Rosalie's eyes rounded in horror. "You, you don't think Cousin Louisa has, has been kidnapped?"

"It looks that way. But no ransom note has been received. I fear very much fear for Mrs Kearny-Pine's life."

Rosalie gasped. "Her life? You mean, you mean she has been murdered? But that's absurd! People like Cousin Louisa don't get murdered. Why should anyone want to murder a perfectly harmless person like Cousin Louisa?"

"You forget, my dear," Miss Joy put in, "that your cousin was wearing her pearls. There's been a lot of talk about those pearls. There was a picture of them in *Life* when she bought them not long ago."

"They were valued at eighty thousand dollars," Mr Magilp went on.

"Eighty thousand dollars is a considerable sum," Professor Bridges remarked drily, "and might well prove a temptation to the criminal mind. I agree with Mr Magilp; the search should be carried farther afield and into more unlikely places than have hitherto been considered."

An unsatisfactory morning was followed by an equally

unsatisfactory afternoon. Towards evening the searchers returned, bringing no information of any kind whatever.

Still another night of anxiety dragged wearily by. Mrs Couch rose early and was at the desk telling Miller to give a very firm "no news" to all kind inquirers, when the hall door opened and a young man, tall, slim and well dressed, came in. He introduced himself as Hubert Pierce, a New York detective sent by Mr Carboy, Mrs Kearny-Pine's lawyer, hoping he could be of assistance to the family. She greeted him with intense relief. Pedro was sent to fetch Mr Greenough from the sitting room where he and Rosalie and Miss Gryce were waiting to go in to breakfast.

"I am thankful you have come," Greenough said as he and Pierce shook hands. "I hoped Mr Carboy would send someone. We need professional help badly. How did you get here so soon?"

"I flew to Santa Fe. Mr Carboy chartered a plane. But the drive here took much longer than it should have, the roads are in bad shape. I suppose I ought to see Mr Pine at once?"

"Mr Pine is out. He left very early to drive to San Carlos, a ranch where he imagined he might get some news. It's a forlorn hope. We are as much at sea as we ever were."

"The police have been notified, I suppose?"

"Oh yes," Mrs Couch answered. "I called up headquarters at Las Rosas yesterday afternoon."

"When was she seen last?"

"At about half past eleven, day before yesterday. We know that she went out for a walk at about that time and that's all we do know. She hasn't been seen since."

"There is a rumour that she went to the curio shop," Mrs Couch put in.

"The curio shop?" Greenough exclaimed. "What does Mr Crowder say to that?"

"He says she hasn't been there for several days. But a woman named Pinto reports having met Mrs Kearny-Pine on Monday and says she asked the way to the curio shop."

"But that's absurd on the face of it," Greenough said. "Mrs Kearny-Pine wouldn't ask the way to the curio shop, she's been there a dozen times."

"Yes. And Mrs Pinto is a notorious liar. But Mr Pierce will want to know what's being said. A Mrs Lopez also insists that she met Mrs Kearny-Pine going towards the Pueblo. And Mrs Lopez is also a liar."

Pierce smiled. "There are ways of persuading liars to tell the truth," he said gently. "That must be Rosalie Colbrook," he went on, glancing through the open door of the living room. "I haven't seen her since she was a child, but I'd know her anywhere. Nobody could forget that exquisite colouring."

"You've said it," Mrs Couch agreed. "What's more, she has common sense and courage as well as looks."

"And the person she is talking to?"

"Miss Gryce, Mrs Kearny-Pine's trained nurse."

He nodded without speaking, watching John Greenough with some interest as the latter turned away to re-join Rosalie in the living room.

She looked up with a smile, and went on to Miss Gryce: "I do wish I had been nicer to Cousin Louisa. But you know how it was, Miss Gryce." Miss Gryce allowed that she did know. "The harder you tried to please her, the less likely you were to succeed. Algy certainly did his best, but he was always rubbing her the wrong way. She wrote to him the day before she disappeared, a scolding letter. She looked as cross as cross when she was writing it. Even Cousin Steve's awfully upset now, of course, but they weren't a bit congenial."

A quiet voice broke in. Hubert Pierce was beside her. "You don't remember me," he said, "but I knew you when you were a little girl. I'm Hubert Pierce."

They shook hands. Pierce was introduced to Miss Gryce. She rose and moved away. Pierce sat down. Greenough explained Pierce's presence and Rosalie expressed her gratitude.

"I know Mrs Kearny-Pine very slightly," he remarked. "Tell me. Is she a loveable person?"

"Well, no –" Rosalie hesitated. "Not exactly lovable. Cousin Louisa is frightfully good."

"A fine upright character, what is called a 'New England conscience,' perhaps?"

"Well, yes..."

"And rather intolerant of the follies of youth? That would account for her attitude towards her nephew."

"Algy? Do you know Algy Atwater?"

"No. But I heard you say just now that he never succeeded in pleasing her."

"Algy is a worm. An unutterable worm!"

"If you will forgive my speaking frankly, I gather that he does not feel any real affection for his aunt?"

"Affection! Why, I've heard Algy say a dozen times that he wished Cousin Louisa was dead and buried." She paused abruptly.

"But of course he didn't mean it. Mr Atwater was probably much more attached to his aunt than you realized."

"I dare say," Rosalie agreed perfunctorily, and went in to breakfast.

Miss Gryce was standing at a window in the hall, looking vaguely out into the street. She turned with a start as Pierce spoke.

But his first words, an expression of sympathy for the family, tactfully including herself, put her at her ease. "You must be doubly anxious," he went on, "because of your professional interest."

Miss Gryce raised her handkerchief to her eyes. "I feel all broken up," she gulped. "I'll be the one to get blamed if she dies of a heart attack somewhere out there in those awful lonesome mountains. But it wasn't my fault. I never let her out of my sight if I could help it."

"You found her difficult?"

"I should say so. She was the fretfullest patient I've ever had the handling of and that's saying a good deal. She treated me more like I was a servant than a trained nurse – a graduate of the T. and C. too!" Miss Gryce tossed her head.

"You seem to have been uncommonly obliging."

"Well, you see, her maid died very suddenly a few days ago and I was willing to make a special arrangement because Miss Clara Burleigh, who I came out here with, wasn't going to need me much longer. So I agreed to do more waiting on her than I should of. I'll know better another time."

"Like all your profession, you prefer a serious case. You have had vast experience, I suppose? And yet you can't be over twenty-five, Miss Gryce."

She tucked in her chin with the pleased grimace that is known as 'bridling'. "Twenty-six," she said. "As for experience." She came to a sudden pause. "I guess I'd better go in to breakfast," she went on. "It must be ready by now."

And she walked away, leaving Pierce looking thoughtfully after her.

11

Hubert Pierce was still considering his conversations with Rosalie Colbrook and Janet Gryce – there was food for thought in both interviews – when the Reverend Mr Wurtz came out of the dining room. The clergyman did not seem inclined to talk, but Mr Pierce offered him a cigar and they sat down for a chat. In a few minutes Pierce knew all about Mr Wurtz's little parish, his nervous breakdown and the parochial purse that had given him this delightful trip to the South West, which was almost as good as going to Palestine.

These topics exhausted, Pierce turned the conversation to the strange disappearance of Mrs Kearny-Pine.

Mr Wurtz heaved a gusty sigh. "Very sad. Very sad," he murmured. "The dear lady was a true Christian and will be greatly missed."

"I see you take for granted that she has met with some accident?"

Mr Wurtz sighed again. "It would seem so," he said dolefully.

"Or she may have been lured away," Pierce reflected. "But there is still another possibility, suicide."

"Now that's an idea." Mr Wurtz nodded sadly. "I hadn't thought of that. There was so much talk about her heart I took for granted her heart had given out. I'd hate to think it was suicide, but it does sort of look that way. Such things do happen."

"Even in the best regulated families."

The clergyman laid a solemn hand on Pierce's knee and his voice dropped to a whisper, "As it happens, I am in a position to know more than most about Mrs Kearny-Pine's family life, and I tell you that family was not well regulated. No sir, it was not!"

"You don't say so!"

"Mrs Kearny-Pine and I had some heart-to-heart talks. But I got a side light on the situation before I ever met the poor lady. You see, Mr Pine and I got acquainted in the train on the way out. We were real congenial." Mr Wurtz smiled. "But at Chicago livelier company came aboard, and I was obliged to retire."

"A lady, I presume. Was she an old friend?"

"That I could not say. But he called her Arabella."

"You are a close observer," Pierce remarked admiringly. "You didn't catch the lady's last name by any chance? Or discover her destination?"

"I did." Mr Wurtz leaned back complacently, thumbs tucked in the armholes of his clerical vest. "I am, as you say, a close observer. The lady's name was Mrs Larkin of New York City and she was booked for Santa Barbara. They were much too intimate," he ended primly.

After further observations on marriage and morals, the clergyman departed. Pierce took a notebook out of his pocket and made a few entries.

"Rosalie Colbrook. Nice girl. Eliminate.

"John Greenough. Seems OK. Rosalie may be an heiress and he may know it.

"Atwater. Probably harmless. But why did Mrs K.P. send him a 'scolding letter'?

"Wurtz. Find out if the Bishop's clerical crook is still at large.

"Janet Gryce. Suspicious. Wire T. and C. Hospital.

"Stephen Pine. Nicknamed 'Tiger' at college. Wire Santa Barbara, re: Arabella Larkin."

He slipped the book into his pocket and strolled to the desk where the clerk was sitting alone, yawning.

"Mr Miller, you are in a position to know everything that goes on in the hotel," he said in a confidential undertone. "And no doubt you see much that would escape a person less observant than yourself."

Mr Miller agreed that he was, and did.

"Therefore," Pierce dropped his voice, "I propose to take you into my confidence. So far, that is, as professional etiquette will permit."

Miller's pale face flushed with elation. "To begin with, I may as well tell you that Mrs Kearny-Pine's family are afraid that she is dead."

"You don't say!"

"Yes, that is the conclusion they have come to, and I agree with them. As you have probably guessed, I am here in a professional capacity. I am a detective."

"You don't say!"

"You belong to what I call the detective type, Mr Miller. Alert, intuitive, with great facial control – that is, you have a poker face – and you are able to keep your own counsel if need be."

The clerk agreed that he had always been like that, and stroked his moustache.

"Let us make an experiment. Are there any letters for Mrs Kearny-Pine and her family in their box?" Miller nodded, remarking he guessed the family had been too upset to ask for the mail. "I want you to look them over – merely at the envelopes, of course," Pierce went on, "and tell me what you can deduce from the outside."

Miller took a dozen letters from the box and laid them on the desk. Pierce indicated the top one. "Now that, for instance?"

"A cinch. Name's on it. Society for the Nourishment of Infant Paupers. One of Mrs Kearny-Pine's charities, I guess. She's had two or three letters from them within the last few days."

"Good." Pierce nodded approvingly. "You have an excellent memory, Miller. Now what about the next one? Addressed to Mr Stephen Pine."

"Well, the postmark is Santa Barbara and it's elegant paper stamped Hotel Miradora. Stylish handwriting too. My guess is, it's a society dame who's writing to Mr P."

"Bravo! Couldn't have done better myself. We can pass over the next two. Abercrombie and Fitch and Bergdorf Goodman, obviously advertisements. What about the pink one for Mrs Kearny-Pine?"

"Postmark Los Angeles. Hm-m-m. Cheap paper, schoolgirl handwriting. Smells of cheap perfume too." The clerk approached the letter to his nose and sniffed disapprovingly, then held it up to the light. "Paper's so thin you can read the name clear through – Myrtle Cream."

Pierce laughed. "I didn't tell you to go that far! But I can tell you one thing, I never found a more promising assistant. Now that's enough about the letters, we'll try another test. Can you tell me what telegrams have recently been received by any members of the family? Telegrams are usually telephoned here from the office, I suppose?"

"A wire came for Mr Pine yesterday, but they didn't phone it. Operator told me he had orders not to... Say, here's a boy with another wire now."

A boy sauntered up to the desk. "For Mr Stephen Pine." Pierce and Miller both looked longingly at the buff envelope. Pierce sighed, the clerk put it into the proper pigeon hole.

"What do I do next, Mr Pierce?"

"Just keep your eyes open and your ears pricked. Remember, I'm depending on you..." He broke off, glanced out of the window. "Here comes Mr Pine."

Making for the stairs, Pine stopped as Pierce's gentle voice said: "Steve, don't you remember me? I'm Tubby Pierce's brother."

"What's that you say?" Steve blinked. "You're Tubby Pierce's brother? Why, Tubby was in my class at College. Damn good fellow, Tubby. So you're Hubert. I remember you now." His face clouded.

"I suppose you've heard about the trouble we're in," he mumbled. "My wife went out for a walk day before yesterday and never came back. We don't know what's become of her."

"So I heard. And I'm sorry, Steve. Terribly sorry."

Steve passed a big gloved hand across his eyes. "I'm about crazy with anxiety, Hubert. Don't know which way to turn, or what to do next..."

"I am here to help you," Pierce said earnestly. "Mr Carboy sent me. I was recommended to him by Bishop Barlow. Mr Carboy thought you ought to have professional assistance."

Steve stared at the floor in gloomy silence, biting his glove. Looks like a bear in that heavy overcoat, Pierce said to himself.

"You can trust me," Pierce went on. "You'll have to get expert advice sooner or later and you'll find it pleasanter to deal with me than with a stranger."

"Maybe you're right," Steve grumbled. "Anyway, if I need professional advice I'll be glad to call you in. But I can't think we've got as far as that just yet. You see, I'm expecting my wife to return any minute..."

"Mr Pine." The clerk approached with an envelope in his hand. "I guess you'll want to see this wire that came for you a minute ago."

Steve took the message and was tearing it open when Rosalie came downstairs.

"Any news, Cousin Steve?" she cried. "Had Cousin Louisa been to San Carlos? Did you find out anything?"

"Not a thing," he muttered, reading the telegram.

"A telegram!" Rosalie exclaimed. "Not from Cousin Louisa?"

Steve frowned. "No, it isn't." He crumpled the paper and stuffed it into his pocket. "Rosalie, this is Mr Hubert Pierce, an old friend of mine."

"Mr Pierce and I have already met," Rosalie smiled.

"I've been telling Mr Pine that I hoped to be allowed to help you all professionally," Pierce said. "As you know, I am a detective."

"We certainly need help," Rosalie sighed. "It's nearly two days now. I feel as if I couldn't bear another minute of this suspense.

Just waiting and listening..."

Steve muttered something under his breath, tore off his overcoat and flung it on a chair. "Damned hot in here," he growled, and sat down heavily. "I'm all in. I never felt so dead beat in all my life!"

"I want to talk things over with you, Steve," Hubert Pierce put in, "but I can wait until you're rested. You'll feel a lot better when you have had a bath and a shave."

"That's right." Steve stumbled to his feet. "See you later then, Hubert. For that matter, Rosalie can tell you anything you want to know as well as I can."

He went upstairs, dragging his feet and leaning on the bannisters. The two looked after him commiseratingly. "Poor Cousin Steve," Rosalie remarked, "he's perfectly exhausted. I'm glad he wants you to help us."

"I'm not sure that he does," Pierce said drily. "I must be off. I'll go to my room first, though, and change. This suit is too warm." He turned to go and paused. "Mr Pine has left his coat, I'd better take it to him." He picked up the coat and went upstairs.

As he reached the upper corridor, he paused, extracted Stephen Pine's telegram from the coat pocket, smoothed it out and read it. It was short enough: "Actions speak louder than words."

Now what does that mean? he said to himself. No signature. Sent from Santa Barbara this morning. He frowned, crumpled the paper and replaced it in the coat pocket. Then he knocked at Stephen Pine's door and handed in the coat. But instead of going to his own room he went downstairs again and betook himself to Mrs Couch's office.

She looked up inquiringly from her desk as he came in.

"I shall want to talk to the staff, Mrs Couch," he said. "When would be the most convenient time for me to do so?"

"Oh, must you?" Mrs Couch wrung her hands. "To my mind, they none of them know any more than you or I do what has become of this unfortunate lady. She's not the only one who's unfortunate, either," she added bitterly. "The Clarks are all leaving. I don't blame them, I'm sure..."

"It's a good deal worse for you than for the guests."

"I should say so. I-I don't know as I ever spent a more trying week. First a death in the house, and then this fuss about Mrs K.P."

"A death? You mean the death of the French maid, I presume. Mr Carboy mentioned that she had died. Tell me about it."

"There's nothing much to tell. The poor woman took an overdose of sleeping medicine and died in the night."

"Was there an inquest?"

"Oh no. It wasn't necessary. Doctor Sylvestro told the authorities it was all as plain as plain could be."

"I see," Pierce nodded. "And you don't, of course, see any connection between the two affairs? You don't think that the death of the maid had anything to do with the disappearance of the mistress?"

"Oh my no!" Mrs Couch was emphatic. "I only meant that it was bad for my business having two disagreeable things come right on top of each other."

"I understand. Well, Mrs Couch, I shan't disturb the staff any more than I can help. I'll postpone questioning them until I have looked over the ground more carefully. Now, Mrs Couch, I want you to tell me how Mrs Kearny-Pine impressed you personally. What are her chief characteristics?"

"That's hard to say." Mrs Couch hesitated. "If you didn't know who she was you'd never look at her twice. She hadn't any characteristics except obstinacy. She was as obstinate as a mule."

"For instance?"

"Well, she took a fancy to that image in the living room, the Blue Santo – the saint the hotel's named for – and pestered me till I sold it to her. And the worst of it is," Mrs Couch smiled ruefully, "I'll have to return the money! When Mr Magilp was here yesterday he examined that image and he says it's a fake, made in..."

"Too bad," Pierce broke in, anxious to return to more essential matters. "But we're getting off the subject. What about your guests? You said just now that the Clarks were leaving. Nothing suspicious about their going so suddenly, I suppose?"

"Oh my no! They come from my home town, Plymouth, Massachusetts. Mr Jabez Clark is the president of the biggest bank in Plymouth and the family are all respectable as can be."

"And the other guests?"

Mrs Couch reflected. "John Greenough has been here more than three months now," she said at length. "And the Plummers from Las Rosas I've known for years," she went on. "The two Miss Burleighs from New York, and old Mrs Rowe and the Cravens are also beyond suspicion. And I have the same feeling about Professor Bridges, who's been here about two weeks, and that little school teacher from Kansas City, Miss Spingle; both of being as quiet and respectable as they can be. She spends her time sightseeing and he's out all day picking flowers. He's crazy about orchids; they say his conservatory is a wonderful sight."

"An expensive hobby, he must be well off."

"I guess so. The Plummers are real wealthy too, made money in oil. They'll be leaving, I dare say," she sighed, "when they hear the Clarks are going."

"And that's the lot?"

"That's the lot. It's so early in the season we're only half full. That's all – except the little parson. He's an ordinary little fellow but quiet enough."

"Oh, he's quiet enough. And after all there's nothing suspicious in being ordinary. I rather think I shall have to look for clues outside the hotel," and Pierce took his departure, leaving Mrs Couch in a somewhat disintegrated condition.

He found Rosalie and John Greenough in the writing room and asked her to tell him about the fright that Mrs Kearny-Pine was reported to have had recently.

"I'm glad you're taking that up," she said. "I have felt all along that Cousin Louisa's disappearance is in some way connected with her visit to that horrid little murder house." She went on to describe the incident in detail.

"Strange," Pierce nodded. "It might be a good idea to search that house."

"That's just what I thought! I made Mr Greenough take me there. We went over it from top to bottom."

"And you saw nothing to justify your suspicions?"

"Not a thing."

"Was that your only attempt at sleuthing?"

Rosalie laughed. "We went to a motor camp to see a rough looking man who was in the curio shop the last time Cousin Louisa and I were there. He turned out to be a perfectly sweet person with the darlingest children, and as honest as the day. So then we went for a climb and we climbed right to the top of Eagle Peak and that came near being the end of me, of both of us! I went too close to the edge and I would have gone over and been killed – the cliff is terribly high you know – if John hadn't caught me just in time!"

"Really? A narrow escape. Nothing to do with the case, however. Well, I'm off now for a bite of lunch. See you later."

Half an hour later, he was crossing the square to the telegraph office where he sent four messages. Two to New York – one to the T. and C. Hospital and the other to Carboy and Patterson; one to Santa Barbara, and one to Los Angeles.

12

But Hubert Pierce's stroll around the village, his prowlings and seemingly casual chats brought in nothing of any value. He returned to the hotel, feeling slightly discouraged, hoping against hope that Mrs Kearny-Pine had come during his absence.

He was disappointed. She had not arrived, and what was almost as bad, the Press had! Only two reporters, and no camera men as yet, their car had broken down just this side of Santa Fe, Miller informed him. But this was, of course, only the beginning.

Pierce could only agree, and was turning away from the desk with a sigh of exasperation, when Rosalie and John Greenough came downstairs.

He suggested a family conference to consider future plans, and asked them to wait for him in the living room while he went to fetch Mr Pine and Miss Gryce.

They obeyed. A window was open, bits of worsted, souvenirs of Mrs Kearny-Pine's embroidery, still littered the living room carpet. Pedro's duties had been neglected during the recent confusion. Rosalie sighed as she moved languidly to an armchair and sat down to wait.

"I wonder if Mr Pierce went to Governor Dane's house," she said, "and, if he did, whether he noticed anything that we didn't see."

"I doubt it. We looked everywhere."

"Could there be a hiding place in the wall? A secret cupboard perhaps?"

"You're picturing that little adobe as a castle in Spain, riddled with oubliettes and secret passages."

"I suppose I am," she agreed wearily. "It's absurd, I know, but

I'm so possessed with the idea that the place holds a secret that when we were there I found myself looking in every little crack and corner for Cousin Louisa! As if we were playing a sort of hide the thimble and Cousin Louisa might be hidden under a table, or a bed, or..."

Rosalie broke off, glanced across the room, drew a quick sharp breath: "The sofa!" she cried. "I never thought of the sofa!" Springing to her feet, she darted across the room and flung her whole weight against the sofa. It was heavy, but before John Greenough could reach her, she had shoved it to one side.

From under it a small grey something the tip of a grey slipper protruded! Rosalie gave a wild scream and tottered backward, would have fallen if Greenough had not caught her in his arms.

"Oh, did you see? Did you see?" she moaned. "She's there! Cousin Louisa, She's there under the sofa! Oh, I can't bear it, I can't bear it!"

And now the room was suddenly full of people; Pedro, Miss Gryce, Hubert Pierce, Mrs Couch. Other bewildered faces looked in over their shoulders from the hall.

"What is it?" Pierce demanded. "What has happened?"

Greenough pointed to the sofa and the grey foot, murmuring to Rosalie, "Don't look, my dear. Don't look." And he stood between Rosalie and the sofa as Pedro stepped forward.

"Wait!" Pierce called Pedro back. "Shut the door, Mrs Couch."

Mrs Couch gave one shuddering glance at the sofa, waved back the spectators, and shut the door in their inquisitive faces.

"Now, Pedro," Pierce went on. "Help me to push the sofa away. Go slow, don't hurry."

The two men bent, pressed their shoulders against the sofa, inch by inch it moved, slid away, and disclosed a crumpled grey bundle huddled together. A body, a dead body, the dead body of Mrs Kearny-Pine. She lay on her back, her face partly covered by a grey silk scarf wound tightly around her head and shoulders. Across her feet her grey coat and hat and her parasol were bunched together as if they had been thrust in hurriedly.

For a long moment they stood looking down in silence; a sick silence broken only by the sound of Rosalie's weeping. Then:

"Poor thing, poor thing," Mrs Couch murmured, wiping her eyes. "How could anyone have had the heart?" She paused with an exclamation of dismay as the door was dashed open and Stephen Pine burst into the room.

He pushed forward, elbowing his way through the group that instinctively tried to shield him from the thing that lay at their feet, and looked down. He groaned, and with a muttered "Lulu! Poor little Lulu! I didn't mean it. Forgive me! Forgive me!" he staggered to a chair, let himself drop, hid his face in his hands and sat shaking from head to foot with loud gulping sobs.

"Get him upstairs, Miss Gryce," Pierce whispered. "I want to clear the room."

He motioned to Greenough, who nodded understandingly and touched Rosalie. She rose obediently. In a few minutes the room was empty except for Pierce, Mrs Couch and Pedro.

At a suggestion from Pierce, Mrs Couch dispatched Pedro to the housekeeper's room; he returned with a white linen sheet.

"Don't tell anyone what's happened, Pedro, until I come out," Pierce said as he took the sheet. "Try to keep them quiet out there, Mrs Couch," he went on, as she too turned to go. "None of them really saw anything. Let them go on guessing as long as you can."

Mrs Couch, white faced and anxious, turned to the door. As she opened it, a buzz of eager questioning met her, and could still be heard after she had closed it behind her.

And now Hubert Pierce was alone and free to begin his examination.

He bent close over the body, considering every minutest detail, and made careful notes of position and appearance. Then he drew a small camera from his pocket and took several photographs from different angles. Another fifteen minutes were spent in a survey of the room, ending with the sofa and a small table that stood in front of it. The surface of this last was marred by a sticky circle; he touched it, licked his finger, and concluded that the mark came from a glass of milk. And still he had not touched the body.

How was it done? Pierce asked himself, as, at length, he closed his note book and stood looking down at the crumpled figure at his feet.

He hesitated for a moment, then, kneeling, he slipped his hand under the body. His groping fingers encountered something soft – a cushion – and through its bulk he could feel a rigid object.

"Stabbed!" he muttered. "That's the hilt of a knife. No blood on the floor. How does that happen?"

The cushion, he realized at once, was the explanation. The scarf had been used to bind the cushion over the woman, and the cushion, serving as a sponge, had sopped up the blood that might otherwise have trickled out from under the sofa in a betraying river. Not a bad idea, Pierce said to himself – must be a clever fellow.

A low knocking interrupted his train of thought. He spread the sheet over the body, went to the door, and opened it a crack.

It was Mrs Couch. "The sheriff from Las Rosas is here," she whispered.

"Does he know about the murder?" Pierce asked, as he joined her in the hall, locking the door of the living room behind him.

"No; he's only just come. And none of the guests really know any thing either, though they're just crazy to find out what's going on. But I've managed to hush them up and get the hall cleared."

The hall was empty except for Miller the clerk and a stout red faced man who stood at the desk, holding forth in a loud hearty voice. He turned, as Pierce and Mrs Couch approached, and stretched out an enormous hand.

"Glad to meet you," he roared, as Pierce was introduced. "My name's Bill Bustard. Glad to meet you. I've heard tell of you. I don't guess I'm greatly need here. Though I wouldn't wonder if a greenhorn wasn't about as good as a high tone New York detective when it comes to chasing a lady who's bent on playing hide and seek! As I was saying to Miller just now, I bet my bottom dollar she'll turn up brisk as you please, before..."

"The body of Mrs Kearny-Pine," Hubert Pierce broke in impatiently, "has just been found."

"What the devil!" Bustard's jaw dropped in astonishment. "You mean she's dead?"

"Yes. She is dead."

"Suicide?"

"No. She was murdered."

"Where? How?"

"In that room." Pierce indicated the door of the living room. "The body was found under a sofa. She has been stabbed with a knife."

"Let's have a look!" Bustard moved eagerly towards the closed door. He and Pierce went in together and shut the door behind them.

Mr Bustard's exuberance left him as Pierce drew aside the sheet and the small crumpled figure was disclosed.

"You must of touched the corpse," he said suspiciously. "Or how'd you know she was stabbed? You'd no call to do that. You know damn well you'd ought to of waited till I got here!"

"Nothing has been disturbed," Pierce said smoothly. "All is exactly as I found it. I have only slipped my hand under the body. But I should not have done even that if I had been perfectly sure that you were coming, Mr Bustard."

"That's right," Bustard grunted, mollified by Pierce's manner. "But I came as quick as ever I could, considering the God awful roads. Let's turn the body over now and make sure."

Bustard removed the coat and hat and parasol. With slow care the body was turned over on its side. Pierce had guessed right; the scarf bound a large blue silk cushion over the wound. When the cushion, stained with dried blood, was drawn way, the bone hilt of a knife became visible.

Bustard stood up and glanced around the room. "I suppose you've looked everything over about as good as I could of myself," he remarked. "I see you've took some photos." The camera stood on a table. "Any fingerprints? You didn't handle the knife, of course?"

"No, I haven't touched the knife. But if the murderer left any fingerprints, which no up to date criminal would dream of doing they would have been washed away. The hilt is encrusted with dried blood."

"That's right. We'll leave the knife where it is for the present. The doctor will want to have a squint at it. It looks to me like it was a common sort of knife, not much of a clue." He replaced the covering sheet. "What do you figure was the reason for the crime, Mr Pierce?"

"Mrs Kearny-Pine was wearing a valuable string of pearls," Pierce said slowly. "The pearls are gone."

"So they are! Just a plain case of robbery then." Bustard looked disappointed. "Not much mystery about that. And we'd ought to find the feller pretty easy in a little place like Tecos."

"I'm not so sure," Pierce demurred. "He's had a good start. Two days. She was seen last at about eleven, day before yesterday. Several persons including her young cousin, Miss Colbrook saw her at that hour, sitting on the sofa in this room, embroidering. When Miss Colbrook returned, at a few minutes before one o'clock, she was surprised to find her cousin was no longer here. As Mrs Kearny-Pine's outdoor garments had disappeared from her room, it was taken for granted that she had gone out for a walk. In fact, I was told that she had gone out by so many persons and with such conviction that I took the walk for granted. Which was exceedingly stupid of me. I should have taken nothing for granted."

"Oh well, we all make mistakes. Suppose the fellow hid the clothing to make it look like she'd gone out, and gain time?"

"Obviously. The coat and hat must have been stolen from her

bedroom not long before the murder. Miss Gryce, the trained nurse, had left them lying on the bed ready for Mrs Kearny-Pine to put on in case she decided to go out."

"Looks like it was somebody who'd have access to the rooms upstairs. Some of the help maybe. But don't it strike you this was a mighty public place to choose?"

"Not so very public. No one could look in from the street, for the window panes are of stained glass. There is only one door, and the lady would have had her back to it as she sat on the sofa. A man could have slipped up behind her unseen, and unheard on this thick carpet. Elderly ladies are apt to be deaf."

"You'd thought she'd of let out a yell, and there must of been folks in the hall."

"Not at that hour. I understand that guests usually spend the morning visiting points of interest in the neighbourhood. And the servants would have been at dinner. The murderer probably closed the door when he came in."

"He must have been an awful speedy worker!"

"It was a matter of minutes. The back of the sofa is low. The murderer waited until the lady bent forward, perhaps to take something off of the stand – that circular mark suggests a glass of milk. Then he struck."

"And the knife was left in the wound so as to stop a gush of blood."

"Just so. And he trusted to the cushion to act as a sponge. The long fringe of the sofa touches the floor and would hide anything that was under it. Death was probably instantaneous. She was stabbed, bound up in the scarf and cushion and rolled under the sofa. The garments previously taken from her room were also shoved in. And the thing was done."

"Well, the feller made a mighty neat job of it," Bustard grunted. "I guess I'd better get busy. First off, I'll phone my office and tell 'em to have the trains watched, and get Doc Quinby here quick as ever they can. And I'll send some smart men out over the likeliest mountain trails. And then," Bustard drew a long breath, "I better get the help lined up and put 'em through the third degree."

"They are all locals."

Bustard grinned. "That suits me. There ain't a man in the Southwest can learn me how to handle 'em. And when I've turned the help inside out, I'll have a word with the guests. Check their alibis, and so forth. As for the family, I'll be obliged if you'll tell 'em I need to ask a few questions."

They left the room. Bustard locked the door and joined Mrs Couch, anxiously awaiting him at the desk. Pierce went upstairs.

A knock at Steve's door brought no answer. Pierce went in, found the room darkened and Steve lying face down on the bed. He gulped a fretful "What do you want? Can't you leave me alone?"

"I'm afraid I can't, Steve," Pierce said gently. "The sheriff from Las Rosas is here and he wants to see you. He won't keep you long."

"Why can't you tell him what he wants to know?"

"I'll tell him all I can, of course. Although, as a matter of fact, Steve, you have never formally engaged me. Do you want me to take charge of the case?"

"Yes, of course."

"I'll do my best. This is a shocking affair, Steve. I needn't tell you how."

"Don't talk about it," Steve burrowed his face still farther into the pillow.

"But it's got to be talked about," Pierce protested. "There will have to be an inquest, of course."

Steve raised a swollen face, red and tear-stained. "An inquest?" he groaned.

"An inquest is unavoidable. And there's the funeral to arrange."

"The funeral!" Steve buried his face again. "What the devil do I know about funerals? Ask Rosalie. Tell Rosalie to see about it."

"Don't you think Rosalie is rather young to tackle that sort of thing, and she's had a bad shock."

"And what about me? Haven't I had a shock? Haven't I?"

"Pull yourself together, Steve," Pierce broke in. "This is no time to give way to grief. The sooner you see the sheriff, Mr Bustard, and get it over, the better."

"All right." Steve reared himself up and sat disconsolately on the side of the bed. "All right. Where do I see this Buzzard?"

"The name is Bustard. You can talk to him in the writing room. But you'd better wash your face and brush your hair, Steve, before you go down. You're a sight."

As they reached the hall, Miller beckoned to Pierce, holding up several envelopes. Steve went on into the writing room. "Telegrams for you, Mr Pierce," the clerk remarked hopefully.

"Thanks."

To Miller's disappointment, Pierce slipped the envelopes into his pocket unopened. "Where is Mr Bustard?"

"In the kitchen with Mrs Couch. Raising hell, if you ask me," Miller sniffed.

"*Our* methods are more subtle," Pierce smiled. "Here he comes now."

The pantry door burst open and Mr Bustard advanced across the dining room, swabbing his face with a bandanna handkerchief. He growled.

"You didn't learn anything?" Pierce asked.

"Not one damn thing."

"I gave Mr Pine your message. He is waiting for you in the writing room, the little room at the foot of the stairs. He is exceedingly anxious to give you any information that may help you to track down the criminal. But of course he's terribly cut up. This ghastly tragedy has been almost too much for him. You'll make your questioning as brief as possible, I hope?"

"I sure will. Say, Pierce, you better come along. These big bugs from the East get me all fussed up."

Pierce saw with relief that Steve had succeeded in pulling himself together. His perfunctory: "How d'you do – much obliged to you for coming," cut off Bustard's expression of sympathy half way. Without attempting to shake hands, Bustard sat down at a desk and prepared to write.

"Your name, sir?" he began deprecatingly. "And residence?"

"Stephen K. Pine. New York."

"Your business?"

"I am not in business."

"What may your occupation be, then?"

"I play polo, shoot big game in Africa and the Rocky Mountains, and amuse myself in various other ways. Suppose we agree that I am what is called a gentleman of leisure and leave it at that."

"All right," Bustard grunted. "And now, Mr Pine, I'm awful sorry if it makes you feel bad, but I'm obliged to put some questions about the deceased. I got her name – Louisa Kearny Pine. Is that right?"

"It is."

"And her residence was the same as yours, I presume?"

"It was," Steve answered stonily. "For some years past we have lived at 860 Fifth Avenue. This winter my wife decided on this Western trip and she – we – closed our house and I took an apartment on Park Avenue."

"Her age and birthplace?"

"She was born in Barton, New Jersey. As for her age, I don't remember exactly. I think she was about fifty-seven."

"By the way, Mr Pine," Bustard glanced over his notes, "I guess you didn't give me your age."

"I am forty-nine," Steve answered, biting his lips.

"There was quite some difference in your ages then?"

"Obviously. It would not seem to require any very great mathematical genius to make that computation."

"Now look here, Mr Pine," Bustard protested. "You don't need to act so sarcastic with me. I got to ask you these questions, and you got to answer 'em. See."

"What else do you want to know?"

"The deceased was a wealthy woman, I understand."

"She was. My wife inherited a large fortune from her father, Myron C. Bentley, and it has increased considerably since his death. The management of her estate is in the hands of her lawyers, Messrs. Carboy and Patterson of 60 Wall Street. Mr Carboy is probably on his way here now. He can give you whatever information you need."

"I see. And you have been married how long?"

"Twelve years."

"No children?"

"No children."

"Your married life has been happy, I presume?"

Steve reddened, but he got out a choked "Absolutely. My wife was a very fine woman."

"No reason you can suggest for anyone wishing to harm her? Blackmail? Or anything of that sort?"

"Damn you, what do you mean by that!" Steve heaved himself up in the chair, glaring. "My wife was..."

"Keep calm, Steve," Pierce put in. "Mr Bustard is only doing his duty."

"Then what do you reckon was the reason for the crime?"

"The reason?" Steve roared, smiting the arm of his chair with a clenched fist. "The reason? Great God Almighty. Isn't the reason as plain as a pikestaff? She was killed for her pearls."

"Just so. That is precisely my theory."

"Then why in God's name do you keep on badgering me with your fool questions? Why don't you get out and *do* something, instead of..."

Bustard rose. "That will do – for the present, Mr Pine," he said drily, and gathering his papers together, he left the room.

"Damned impertinent a fellow as ever I saw," Steve growled. "Though I suppose I oughtn't to have let him get under my skin."

"Don't worry, old man," Pierce said reassuringly, "everything will straighten out all right," and left him.

Pierce would have liked to go on to his own room and open the envelopes burning unread in his pocket. But he couldn't risk keeping Bustard waiting.

13

Pierce had felt a little sorry for Steve. He felt ten times as sorry for Rosalie. Bustard evidently shared Pierce's feeling of compassion. His manner verged on the fatherly, as he said:

"I'm sorry to intrude, ma'am, and I won't keep you a moment longer'n I can help. Just let me have your name, age and place of residence, and your relationship to the deceased."

She got through these questions steadily enough. But when Bustard came to more intimate details, her voice shook. It was with an effort that she explained:

"I did not live with my cousin. I only spent the holidays at her house. My parents are dead and, until lately, I have been at boarding school."

"Were you her guest on this Western trip?"

"Oh yes. I have no money of my own. Cousin Louisa paid for me at St. Timothy's and gave me a dress allowance, and she never forgot my birthday. I-I was very grateful to her."

"Were you pleased when she asked you to come West with her?"

"I was delighted. It seemed too marvellous that I was going to see the West at last! Of course – I never imagined – never imagined that our trip would – would end in such a dreadful, dreadful way!"

"It sure was an awful mean way for a lady to come to her death, ma'am. Do you reckon it was the pearls the murderer was after?"

"I suppose so. Though it seems incredible that anybody could be so wicked."

"There's plenty bad men around, ma'am, even out here in our great Western country. But more'n likely this feller followed you all from New York. You didn't notice any suspicious characters hanging about whilst you was travelling, I suppose?"

"I don't recall anything of the sort. Nobody on the train could have known we had the pearls. They were in my cousin's jewel case and Marie always carried that herself."

"Marie?"

"My cousin's maid, Marie Leclair. She died suddenly, soon after we arrived here, from an overdose of sleeping medicine."

Bustard nodded. "I remember. Dr Sylvestro phoned us everything was OK and we didn't need to investigate. What about after you got here? Noticed anyone acting queer here in Tecos?"

"No, except that my cousin had a fright not long ago." She turned to Pierce. "I told you about that."

"You had better tell Mr Bustard too," Pierce said.

So Rosalie described that first strange visit to Governor Dane's house and her own subsequent search.

"I'll have a talk with that lot on the off-chance. Now, Miss Colbrook, only one more question: What terms would you say the deceased and her husband was on? Would you say they was a happy couple?"

"Why – I suppose so..." Rosalie hesitated.

"Did you ever hear any spatting?"

"They – they sometimes had arguments," Rosalie acknowledged. "The day that Mr Pine arrived here – he didn't come West with us, but later – something must have happened to annoy him, for he seemed rather cross. But Cousin Louisa wasn't... Oh, it seems so unkind to say it... but Cousin Louisa wasn't easy to live with."

"I see. Well, I guess I better have a talk with Miss Gryce now. Her room is on this floor?"

"Number twenty-four, almost next to this."

"Right. So it's your opinion, Miss Colbrook, that if there did come a family jar now and then, it was as much the lady's fault as the gent's?"

Pierce saw that Bustard was slightly disappointed at the finality of her: "I certainly do think so!"

"A right sweet little girl," Bustard said, as Pierce joined him in the corridor, "pretty as flowers in May and as good as she's pretty. Number twenty-four? Here we are."

"I want to get a notebook from my room," Pierce remarked, as Bustard knocked at Miss Gryce's door. "I'll be with you in a minute. By the way, you'd better leave the door open."

"That the sort she is?" Bustard grinned.

"You never can tell," Pierce smiled, and went on down the corridor.

At a safe distance, he took from his pocket the telegrams that had been waiting so long unread and tore open the first that came to hand. It happened to be the one he wanted most, from the T. and C. Hospital in New York.

"No Janet Gryce graduated here," the message ran, "if Jane Greer was intended regret to say she is wanted by N. Y. police."

Now that, Pierce said to himself, may mean very little or it may mean *everything*! He stuffed the other telegrams back into his pocket – there was no time for them now – and hurried back to Miss Gryce.

Bustard and Miss Gryce were already on good terms, Pierce saw. Both were laughing. She gave Pierce a sidelong look as he came in, and was at once serious. Bustard sat up with a brisk: "Well, let's get down to business. Name? Married or single?"

"My name is Janet Gryce and I am not married."

"Nor divorced?"

"Nor divorced."

"Residence?"

"I was born in Buffalo, but for the past few years I have been living in New York City."

"Present address?"

It seemed to Pierce that she made a perceptible pause before the answer came: "239 East Seventeenth Street."

"You are a graduate of what hospital?"

"Of the T. and C. The Hospital for Tubercular and Crippled, in New York. Since my graduation, I have been doing private nursing."

"What can you tell us about the deceased? This Mrs Kearny-Pine, as she called herself – sort of queer she hadn't just the same name as her husband. What sort of a woman was she?"

"Didn't know her very well. I had only been with her a few days, just since her maid died."

"No reason you know of why anybody would want to get rid of her?"

"No indeed! You don't mean to imply that she was not killed by a robber? Her pearls were very valuable, and –"

"I know all about her pearls," Bustard put in irritably. "And that's all I do know as yet. Tell me, Miss Gryce, would you say those two was a happy married couple?"

Miss Gryce reflected for a moment. Then: "Do I have to answer that question?" she asked.

"Miss Gryce's delicacy does her credit, Bustard," Pierce remarked, "and should be respected. Unless you feel this line of inquiry is absolutely necessary."

"I'm the best judge of what's necessary and what isn't," Bustard snapped. "Go ahead, Miss Gryce; answer my question. Do you, or do you not, think those two was a happy couple?"

"Since you insist," Miss Gryce pursed her lips. "Since you insist, I must admit that Mrs Kearny-Pine and her husband fought like cats and dogs."

"You don't say!"

"They did indeed. The evening Mr Pine arrived here he was in an awful temper. He didn't come West when she did and she sent for him. That very evening they quarrelled something fierce. Why, Miss Colbrook and me could hear him roaring at her right here in this room!"

"What did you reckon was the cause of the row?" Bustard demanded.

"I couldn't say exactly. But I sort of gathered he hadn't wanted to come West. I guess they was both of 'em making mountains out of molehills, like husbands and wives always do. One thing seemed to make him awful mad was the room she'd engaged for him. He said it wasn't good enough – it's at the back and right over the kitchen and she must have said she wanted to have him in the room next to hers at night – though I was next to her on the other side – for he began grumbling about her snoring keeping him awake... And they had it back and forth about that for quite a while. And he ended up with: 'All right, Louisa, have it your way. Leave the door open. But remember, if I hear so much as one snore I'll come in and shoot your head off!'"

There was a second's dead silence. Then Bustard remarked: "That's pretty interesting, isn't it, Pierce?"

Pierce laughed. "It would be more interesting if I didn't happen to know that Stephen Pine's bark is a lot worse than his bite, and I fancy Miss Gryce realizes that as well as I do."

He gave her a sympathetic smile. "I suppose, Miss Gryce, that family jars often increase the difficulties of your arduous profession. Such experiences, for a young girl like yourself, must be exceedingly painful. You don't look more than eighteen, though you told me you were twenty-six. No one would imagine you had been out of the training school for more than six months at most!"

"I graduated three years ago."

"Really! Three years ago? Then you must have been in the same class at the T. and C. with a friend of my sister's. I wonder if you knew her? Jane Greer, a very nice girl, I believe, though I never met her. My sister was much attached to her."

"Jane Greer?" Miss Gryce said considering, and Pierce – listening intently – could detect no tremor in her even voice as she went on "Why no. I don't seem to remember any girl of that name. But of course it was a pretty large class."

"Of course," Pierce nodded. "By the way – to return to that little domestic misunderstanding you were describing just now. I don't suppose, Miss Gryce, that you, for one moment, took Mr Pine's threat seriously."

He gazed fixedly at Miss Gryce, and was interested to see a certain rigidity creep into her attitude. Her clasped hands tightened until the knuckles were white. But she managed a laughing: "Of course not. I knew Mr Pine was only joking."

"I fancy that's about right," Pierce nodded. "By the way, those are extremely pretty moccasins you are wearing, Miss Gryce. Did you buy them in Tecos?"

"They were a present," she said. "I tied up a cut for a boy at the Pueblo, and his grandfather gave them to me."

The answer came readily enough. But Pierce added another black mark to Miss Gryce's record – Mrs Kearny-Pine had been killed by a soft-stepping person.

He glanced at his watch. "I must be going," he exclaimed. "There are several little matters I must attend to before the doctor arrives. Are you coming, Bustard?"

Bustard rose, but reluctantly. The two men left the room together. But having got Bustard away from Miss Gryce, Pierce excused himself on the plea of making a few notes and went on to his own room, deep in thought. *Jane Greer* and *Janet Gryce* – the similarity was striking. And he had caught the nurse in one direct lie; no Janet Gryce had been graduated from the T. and C. And Miss Gryce was a soft-stepping person. Yes; Pierce said to himself; so far, Miss Gryce was his best bet.

In his room at last, he sat down to examine the telegrams with more than a little interest. But the first, from Santa Barbara, was disappointing: "Mrs Arabella Larkin at Miradora prominent socially stop appears wealthy stop Reno divorce last winter."

Not much in that, he reflected. A divorce doesn't size a woman up nowadays as it would have fifty years ago. But I wish that little parson hadn't seen Steve and Mrs Larkin together on the train. He sighed as he laid down the Santa Barbara telegram and took up another.

It was from the police station in Los Angeles: "Myrtle Cream well known in sporting circles here has worked at Hollywood out of job at present but appears flush stop more information shortly."

Pierce was going on to examine the one remaining telegram when a sudden thought struck him, and he paused. The connection between Myrtle Cream and the murder might not be so remote after all! Suppose the pink letter he and Miller had examined was not the first communication Mrs Kearny-Pine had received? Suppose the Myrtle Cream correspondence had been the cause of the break between Mrs Kearny-Pine and her nephew, Algy Atwater? Carboy had mentioned a letter recently received from Mrs Kearny-Pine which suggested she was fed up with Algy's extravagance and was about to cut him out of her will. And Rosalie Colbrook had spoken of a note that Cousin Louisa had asked her to deliver at Algy's studio a few hours before the murder. A scolding letter, Rosalie had called it. Suppose that scolding letter reproved Algy for some recently discovered scandal – discovered through an appeal from Myrtle Cream for money, or a threat of blackmail – and announced an intention of disinheriting him? Suppose Algy, on receipt of the scolding letter, had hurried around to the hotel...

A fact suddenly struck Pierce – where had Algy been during these last eventful days? Pierce couldn't recall hearing him mentioned as taking any part in the search for his aunt, of having visited distant ranches, or helped to drag the pond. Strange. Pierce went to his telephone and called the desk:

"That you, Miller? Pierce speaking. Has the doctor come yet?... Well, give me a ring when he turns up. Where is Mr Bustard?... More reporters? Of course... No; I'll leave the gentlemen of the press to Mr Bustard for the time being. But there's a man I do want to talk to, Mr Algy Atwater. He isn't around the hotel anywhere, I suppose?... Hasn't been in today? How lately have you seen him? Was he here day before yesterday?... He was? In the latter part of the morning? Then the sooner I have a talk with him the better... He hasn't got a telephone? Then I want you to send Pedro over to Mr Atwater's studio with a message from me. Pedro is to tell him he is badly needed here, and must come at once. Get Pedro off and then come back to the phone. I'll hold the wire... Pedro has gone? Quick work. Are you alone? Good. But keep your voice down; this is between you and me. I want to know what became of those letters you and I looked over yesterday... Miss Gryce took them? You don't know what Miss Gryce did with them, of course... I see. Did any more mail come for Mrs Kearny-Pine today?... No, advertisements can wait. Much obliged, and that's all just now, Miller. The less said about all these little matters the better, you understand... Good boy. I'll be down in a few minutes."

Pierce hung up the receiver, and opened the remaining telegram with some eagerness. If it proved to be the answer to his wire to Carboy and Patterson, asking about Mrs Kearny-Pine's will, it would throw light on Algy Atwater's hopes and fears. It was.

"Kearny-Pine fortune," it ran, "left one half to husband one quarter to Atwater one eighth to Colbrook remainder to charities."

As he went downstairs, Bustard and five young men were crossing the hall to the front door; reporters, of course. It was risky leaving them to Bustard. But at that moment Pedro came in, and Pierce let Bustard go without him.

Pedro had found Mr Atwater's studio locked up, and nobody had answered the bell. Paquita, the Indian girl, had probably gone to the Pueblo for the chief's funeral, but Manuel must be somewhere around the village. Pedro offered to find him, and departed.

"Has Mr Atwater got a car of his own, Miller?" Pierce asked.

"No. Just hires from the garage."

"Call up the garage then, and ask if he's taken out one of theirs lately."

Miller obeyed; gave Pierce a startled glance and exclaimed: "Mr

Atwater motored to the junction a little after twelve day before yesterday; He drove himself."

"The devil he did! Here, let me talk to them." Pierce snatched the receiver.

"Did Mr Atwater take any luggage?" he demanded. "Thank you."

He rang off, and called again: "Central, give me the railway station at the junction," he snapped. "And look sharp!" With the receiver at his ear, he murmured to Miller: "I see Bustard coming in. Tell him I want him, and hold back the reporters if you can."

"The junction? This is Hubert Pierce speaking. I am the detective in charge of the Kearny-Pine murder case. I want to know what passengers left the junction day before yesterday for the West... No matter about the ladies. Was the young man well dressed? The one with the pigskin bag?... Where was he booked for?... Much obliged."

Again he rang off, and spoke: "Long distance, please. I want police headquarters at Los Angeles... You'll call me? Right!"

He hung up, and found Bustard at his elbow, listening eagerly.

"What's up?" Bustard demanded. "What's the dope?"

"I don't know whether its important or not," Pierce said, "but I've just discovered that Mrs Kearny-Pine's nephew, Mr Algy Atwater, left Tecos on the morning of the murder, apparently in a hurry, and took the night train from the junction for Los Angeles."

"Say, how did you..." Bustard began, and broke off as the telephone rang.

"Hubert Pierce speaking. Is that you, Brigham?... Yes; the Kearny-Pine murder case. I wired you yesterday about a girl named Myrtle Cream. No, I don't want her, but I want a man who may turn out to be a friend of hers, Mr Algy Atwater. An artist who has a studio here in Tecos. It seems he left for Los Angeles day before yesterday in the night train from the junction, and I want him followed when he arrives. He's the only young man who took that train who was well dressed and carried a large pigskin bag, so it oughtn't to be difficult. In any case, send a man to Myrtle Cream's apartment, as I have a suspicion that's where he will go. When you get him, tell him that his aunt, Mrs Kearny-Pine, has been found murdered, and he's to return here at once. Tell him abruptly, so as to give him a jolt, you understand, and watch how he takes it... No; except that if you find Mr Atwater with Myrtle Cream I'd like to know how *she* takes the news of the murder or if she gives anything away. And, in any case, get all the dope you can about the girl... Thanks, old man!"

He rang off. But before he could speak "Who is this Myrtle Cream?" Bustard demanded.

"A Los Angeles girl that I think may have something to do with Mr Atwater's hurried departure from Tecos," Pierce answered. "But I may be altogether wrong."

"But how did you get to hear about this girl?" Bustard asked suspiciously.

"That's rather a long story, and there are several important points..."

A motor horn sounded outside. An emaciated man in a black coat entered the hall. It was the doctor from Las Rosas. A hush fell on the room.

In dead silence, the door of the living room was unlocked. The doctor, Bustard and Pierce, and the five reporters went in, leaving Miller to gaze at the closed door with wistful eyes.

14

As Hubert Pierce had anticipated, Dr Quinby could tell them very little that he and Bustard had not already guessed. Mrs Kearny-Pine had undoubtedly been murdered, stabbed by a person standing behind her as she sat on the sofa. When the knife was withdrawn it proved to be, as Bustard had said, a knife of the most ordinary description. The kind known as a hunting knife, with a straight blade and bone handle, brand new and very sharp.

When they emerged from the living room, the door was relocked. Bustard and Dr Quinby retired to the writing room, and Pierce was sent upstairs to ask Mr Pine to join them for a conference.

But Pierce found Steve in the same curiously excited condition as when he had left him after the interview with Bustard. Steve refused to come downstairs again, refused to make any suggestions.

"Why can't you let me alone, Hubert! I engaged you to look after this awful affair. Why don't you go ahead and get busy?"

"Then I must have a free foot, Steve. Do you authorize me to proceed with the investigation in any way I see fit?"

"Lord, yes! I tell you I'll go crazy if I have to talk to cops and medical men."

"And am I authorized to look over Mrs Kearny-Pine papers? Open any letters and telegrams that may come for her?"

Steve hesitated, then:

"I guess you'd better. I know I can't face that sort of thing," he groaned.

Pierce was obliged to return to the writing room without him.

"Mr Pine is very sorry not to see you, Dr Quinby," he said, "and he is much obliged to you for coming. But he is still so upset by the tragedy, as is most natural, that he hopes you will excuse him. He asked me to say that he will be satisfied with whatever arrangements you and Mr Bustard and myself think proper to make. No expense is to be spared, and if we are in doubt we are to consult Miss Colbrook, or Mr Atwater when he returns."

"Mr Atwater?" the doctor asked. "Who is he?"

"Mrs Kearny-Pine's nephew. He lives in Tecos, but unfortunately he is away from home at present. Mr Pine hopes that he himself may be spared the terrible ordeal of being present at the inquest."

"Mr Pine, as the husband of the deceased, is the most suitable person to identify the body," the doctor observed.

"He sure is," Bustard agreed. "I don't hardly think it would do to put a thing like that on a girl like Miss Colbrook."

"Miss Colbrook must be kept out of it as much as possible," Pierce agreed. "I am hoping she won't have to appear at the inquest. Mr Atwater can identify, if he returns in time. If not, how would Miss Gryce do?"

"Miss Gryce is the trained nurse, Doc," Bustard explained. "I guess she'd do all right."

This detail settled, Pierce hurried away. Pedro was waiting for him in the hall with a boy, presumably Mr Atwater's servant. But there was another matter that must first be attended to. He ran upstairs and knocked at Miss Gryce's door.

She turned enquiringly as Pierce came in, but showed no emotion as he said, with intentional abruptness:

"Miss Gryce, some letters came for Mrs Kearny-Pine yesterday morning that I want to examine. I have Mr Pine's authority to do so. The clerk says he gave them to you. May I have them, please?"

She rose at once. "I put them on her dressing table," she said, and left the room. Returning, she handed Pierce four letters. He glanced at them, then looked sharply at her. "Weren't there five letters, Miss Gryce? Miller said there were five."

She shook her head. "Mr Miller is mistaken. That's all the

letters that came yesterday. There may be some at the desk now, I forgot to get the mail this morning."

"Miss Gryce, one of the letters that arrived yesterday is missing. And I happen to know from whom it came. Don't you think you would do well to confide in me? Tell me your reason for keeping back this particular letter?"

She flushed and paled with such painful suddenness that he felt sorry for her, but she only muttered: "I don't know what letter you're talking about. That's all the mail that came for Mrs Kearny-Pine yesterday; I put it on her dressing table and I haven't touched it since."

She turned away and stood looking out of the window. Pierce left the room.

So my next telegram goes to the Society for the Nourishment of Infant Paupers, he said to himself, and proceeded to examine the letters he had secured from her.

The one from Santa Barbara addressed to Stephen Pine, he refrained from opening, though he would have liked to do so, and the others were of no interest except that from Myrtle Cream. This proved to be, as he had expected, an appeal for money, and its allusions to Algy would entirely account for Mrs Kearny-Pine's sudden decision to alter her will. Pierce hurried back to the hall.

But the interview with Manuel, Algy's man-servant, was not illuminating, although Manuel was perfectly willing to talk.

At about twelve o'clock on the day of his departure Mr Atwater had returned to the studio; Manuel knew the hour because the bell had rung while he was chopping wood on the patio just before Mr Atwater called him indoors. Mr Atwater had told Manuel that he was going to Los Angeles for a few days, given him the key of the front door, told him to lock up, to feed the dogs and the parrot and take good care of everything until he, Mr Atwater, came home again. Mr Atwater said he would return very soon. A motor had been waiting outside; Manuel had carried out Mr Atwater's bag… Yes, it was a large pigskin bag… Yes; Manuel had been alone in the house when Mr Atwater left. Paquita was out at the market that morning, and then she had gone to the Pueblo to attend the funeral of Wind-from-the-Mountain... No, Mr Atwater had not given Manuel his address in Los Angeles. How did Mr Atwater seem? Why, he had seemed just as usual, except that he had been in a great hurry. He had to hurry if he was going to catch the train for the West.

"I wish we had Mr Atwater's address," Pierce remarked. "Do you know if any letter or telegram came for him summoning him to Los Angeles?"

"I do not know of any."

"And yet he must have received some message. If we could find it, it might give us his address. I'll go back to the studio with you, Manuel, and have a look around for some such letter or telegram."

Manuel demurred. "Mr Atwater might not wish me to let anybody in."

"And you are quite right to be careful. But we need to get in communication with Mr Atwater at once. As you know, his aunt, Mrs Kearny-Pine, has been murdered." Manuel nodded and crossed himself. "And Mr Atwater has not yet heard the terrible news, for he left Tecos before it was known. Now the family want Mr Atwater to return to Tecos immediately so that he can help them make arrangements for the funeral."

Manuel frowned apologetically. "But you, sir, are not the family."

"That's right." Pierce nodded approvingly. "How would it be if I asked Miss Colbrook to come with me to the studio? Miss Colbrook is 'family,' you know."

Manuel's face cleared. There could, of course, be no objection to Miss Colbrook's coming to the studio. She had often been there.

So Pierce went upstairs, knocked at the door of Rosalie's room and explained his errand. Evidently thankful for any excuse that would take her into the open air, she agreed that it was high time Algy made himself useful and got routed out.

They walked along, talking idly, avoiding the subject in both their minds, until Pierce ventured: "During your conversation with Mr Bustard you said that Mrs Kearny-Pine's maid always carried the jewel case when they were travelling. Who took charge of the pearls at night?"

"Marie did. I found the jewel case on the table beside her bed the night she died."

"She died suddenly, I believe, from an overdose of some sedative. Had she given any indication of ill health? Was she robust looking?"

"Yes, she was. Short and stout and red faced and strong as a horse. The French peasant type."

"I see. And after her death who took charge of the jewel case?"

"Cousin Louisa herself. I wanted her to put the pearls in the hotel safe, but she wouldn't. She said she couldn't lose them if she wore them day and night, and no one could get into her room, for she bolted the door and put a chair against it when she went to bed."

As Manuel unlocked the studio door the dachshunds leaped from their cushions and came yapping to meet them and the parrot set up a screaming and fluttering that took both Rosalie and Manuel to its perch.

They were so absorbed in soothing the bird, that neither of them saw Pierce appropriate a pink letter lying on the couch, or followed him when he slipped into the adjoining bedroom and secured another, a paper crumpled into a ball lying in the fireplace. After a little more perfunctory searching they were turning to go when Pierce paused to glance at a large framed photograph that stood on a shelf. "Is this a picture of Algy?" he asked.

"That's Algy. Frightfully flattering, of course. Algy isn't as good looking as that. He has a weak face, hasn't he?"

Back at the hotel the hall was empty. But through the open door of the writing room Pierce saw Bustard deep in conversation with the Reverend Mr Wurtz. He would have joined them at once, for he realized the danger of allowing the clergyman to unbosom himself, but he had not yet examined the papers he had found in Algy's studio. The pink letter was signed with a single initial, but the paper and perfume proved it unmistakably from Myrtle Cream and Pierce smiled with satisfaction as he read:

"I don't guess its any good me writing for you don't ever answer. But I want you should know I have sent a line to that rich aunt you are always gassing about that will make her sit up and take notice. And I have got me a lawyer. If she don't see her way to help me any he says I got an awful good case. So no more at present. M."

Pierce did not wait to gloat over this, but hurriedly smoothed out the other crumpled paper found in Algy's bedroom:

"My dear nephew," he read, "I have received a communication from a person named Myrtle Cream which has given me a shock that may be exceedingly injurious in my precarious state of health. It will scarcely surprise you to learn that I have instructed Mr Carboy to alter my will. Your present allowance will be continued, but you need expect nothing more from me – except my prayers. I do not propose to have my substance wasted in riotous living. Your sorrowing aunt, L. Kearny-Pine."

Pierce gave a long low whistle as he finished this frigid document. He stuffed both letters into his pocket and joined Bustard and Mr Wurtz in the writing room.

"Say, Pierce!" Bustard exclaimed eagerly. "Just listen to this. Mr Wurtz has been telling me something pretty important about your friend Pine! Seems him and Pine came West on the same train... You say Pine had a lady along, Mr Wurtz?"

"He did," Mr Wurtz said primly.

"And the two was as thick as thieves?"

"They were." Mr Wurtz's primness hardened to disapproval.

"Now what do you think of that, Pierce?"

"I don't think anything of it," Pierce said. "I never imagined that Stephen Pine was a model husband. You are a man of the world, Bustard, you must not take Mr Wurtz's communication too seriously. As a clergyman, Mr Wurtz is obliged to condemn what you and I can afford to take more lightly. Mr Wurtz..."

"Look here, Pierce," Bustard broke in impatiently. "All this is beside the point. Mr Wurtz tells me that Pine had a gun in his grip on the train."

"What of that? The murder was committed with a knife."

"I know it was, but taken with that remark about shooting his wife's head off..." He paused, as a tap sounded on the door.

Pedro appeared. "James Rio from the Pueblo is here," he said. "He wishes to speak to Mr Bustard."

Bustard rose at once, as if he had been expecting this visitor, and went out into the hall. Pierce tactfully suggested to Mr Wurtz the propriety of respecting the family of the virtuous Mrs Kearny-Pine.

Mr Wurtz nodded thoughtfully but before he could speak, Bustard returned, and as the latter sat down with a weary, "Lord, how tired I am!" the clergyman left the room.

"But I'm not half as tired as James Rio," Bustard went on. "He's worn out. Seems those crazy Indians have been giving old grandpa a grand funeral, and ain't got him under ground yet."

"I don't suppose James Rio brought any information about the case?"

"Oh, no. He doesn't know anything about it and cares less. He just came to talk to me about the Tecos River dam. The Pueblos all around this neighbourhood are worrying about their irrigation rights and James Rio is trying to straighten things out for me and Connor. Connor is the district attorney. He phoned he'd be here himself tomorrow to see the inquest goes right. I told James Rio to come in again tomorrow evening. Connor will want to have a word with him."

"You have arranged about the inquest?"

"Yep. Two o'clock tomorrow in the big room over Garcia's store, if the coroner can get here by then – he's away. If not, we'll have it the day after. Well, it's late. Guess I'll turn in. Whether or not the district attorney gets here, I see a busy day ahead of me. Picking holes in alibis, for one thing. Did you get anywhere on alibis, Pierce?"

"I did not. To my mind, the lack of alibis is one of the most puzzling features of the case."

"It sure is. Alibis is scarier than hen's teeth round this hotel. One of the servants could have slipped in from the kitchen 'thout anybody noticing. Some of the guests think they was in their rooms, but ain't sure. Some was out, but don't recall just when they got back. Miss Gryce says she was in her room. Mr Pine don't know whether he was in his own room or the writing room, or whether the door was shut or open. Greenough and the girl was playing tennis at Miss Joy's, but he came back here to the hotel for some more balls – he don't know the hour – and they didn't play all morning but went for a walk – they don't know where – and got back about lunch time. Well," he yawned. "I'll have another whack at 'em tomorrow. Good night."

15

When Hubert Pierce woke the next morning his first thoughts turned to the murder knife, now locked up in the hotel safe. It was of a type common in the South-west, but it was brand new, and newness was a clue that might lead in some unforeseen direction. Pierce felt he ought to know more about it before it was produced at the inquest.

The inquest was giving Pierce a good deal of anxiety. Although Rosalie Colbrook, as well as Stephen Pine, had been asked to attend and although Pierce knew he could count on her charm to offset Steve's arrogance, he feared that Bustard might question Steve along the lines suggested by Wurtz's gossip. If that happened the result might be fatal! However, Mr Carboy was expected to arrive in time, for the inquest had been postponed until the following day, and Carboy might be able to control Steve.

The postponement also gave Pierce plenty of time to trace the murder knife. Coming out of the dining room, he saw John Greenough standing beside the hall fire – waiting no doubt for Rosalie to come down to breakfast – and decided to have a talk with him first.

"There are one or two matters I'd like to discuss with you, Greenough," he said. "Let's go up to your room."

"All right," Greenough nodded. He led the way upstairs to the second floor, and opened the door of a large bedroom rather agreeably littered with painting paraphernalia.

"I wanted to ask you about the visit to a motor camp that Rosalie Colbrook mentioned yesterday," Pierce said, as they sat down. "Are you sure that her rough looking man is not worth following up?"

"Dead sure. An honest soul if ever I saw one."

"He's out, then. Now she also spoke of a narrow escape she had had up on some cliff top. Tell me about it."

"That's the most puzzling thing that ever happened to me," Greenough sighed. "I've thought and I've thought and I simply cannot understand how the stool got out there on the edge."

"The stool?"

"My painting stool. You see, Rosalie sat down on it and it broke and she shot right out into space – it was a bit of luck we didn't both go over! Luckily I had hold of her hand, thinking she might feel dizzy."

"And you are puzzled that it broke?"

"Not so much that, though it was all right the last time I used it; the screws holding the legs together might have fetched loose. What I can't understand is how it got where Rosalie and I found it. I know I didn't leave it there on the edge. The first gust of wind would have blown it off. When I finished painting I put it under a bush. I have a good visual memory and, in my mind, I can look at that bush and see the stool tucked away under the branches."

"Why had you left it on the cliff in the first place?"

"A shower came up. I had to hold my canvas very carefully or it would have got wet, and there was my colour box and easel to carry. So I left the stool – *under a bush.*"

"I see. And suppose you had gone up alone – without someone to hold your hand – and sat down on the stool?"

"I'd be dead now. Dashed to pieces! I couldn't by any possibility have saved myself."

"Has it occurred to you," Pierce said slowly, "that if you had an enemy, this would be a nice safe way to get rid of you?"

"But who would want to?" Greenough exclaimed. "I haven't an enemy in the world so far as I know."

Pierce was silent for a moment. Then: "Did Rosalie guess?" he asked. "Did she know you were surprised at finding the stool had emerged from its bush?"

"Oh no. I let her think it was an oversight; she was scared enough as it was. You see, she hadn't much liked the idea of taking that mountain path in the first place because of the Penitentes. But Eagle Peak isn't one of their haunts, and a child at the motor camp had seen an American going up the day before. So we went."

"The Penitentes? I thought they were a religious society, very ascetic and devout."

"Oh, they're ascetic all right – expiate their sins by the most frightful scourgings and what not. They don't like spies, and I believe persons caught watching their Holy Week processions are apt to be roughly handled. Rosalie had an absurd idea that Mrs Kearny-Pine had got into their clutches. Nothing in that, of course."

"You haven't been guilty of spying, I suppose?"

Greenough laughed. "If I hear chanting anywhere in the woods I hurry off in the opposite direction as fast as I can go!"

"And you have never incurred the enmity of the Pueblo?"

"I have not," Greenough laughed again. "I like the Pueblo and the Pueblo likes me. I've become really attached to James Rio; he's a fine fellow."

"You say you have no enemies *that you know of*. Suppose you had seen, or heard, something in connection with the murder of Mrs Kearny-Pine which you have forgotten, but which the murderer would realize was incriminating? You returned here to the hotel that morning to get some tennis balls. You're sure you didn't meet anyone in the hall, or on the stairs?"

"How can I be sure," Greenough sighed. "I wouldn't have noticed anyone who was staying in the hotel, if I had met them."

"Of course not. Now I want you to think still further back," Pierce went on. "Think back to the death of Marie the maid."

"What!" Greenough exclaimed. "Are you suggesting that her death might have been in some way a prelude to the murder?"

"It's a possibility worth considering. Now, think back. Can you recall any occurrence, no matter how trivial, in connection with

Marie Leclair just before or at the time of her death?"

"Why, no. I scarcely knew the woman... Wait a minute! There was something. It seemed rather odd at the time, but I'd forgotten all about it and I can't think it's important..."

"Let's have it, anyway."

"Well, I happened to be in that vacant room next to hers – Mrs Couch gave me the key because I thought of painting the market-place and I wanted to see if you got a good view of it from there – and I heard voices in the corridor and then in Marie's room. I heard Marie say: 'Thank you so much. I shall enjoy it extremely,' and I left, feeling a little uncomfortable – eavesdropping isn't much in my line – and hurried past Marie's door without glancing at it. But I couldn't help seeing her in the doorway, and she must have seen me; for she gave an embarrassed sort of laugh and said something I didn't catch. I was too far off by that time."

"You didn't see whether the other person was a man or a woman? Or recognize the voice?"

"No; Marie's stout figure blocked the doorway. And the other person spoke in an undertone. But that embarrassed laugh made me think her friend was a man – Lost Arrow, or Pedro, perhaps. Mrs Kearny-Pine would have disapproved of followers."

"I agree. But I wish you had been less punctilious, Greenough. However, what you did see and hear confirms my suspicion that Marie's death ought to be more thoroughly investigated. If I can link it to the murder –"

Pierce took a notebook from his pocket and sat silent, absorbed in rereading and adding to its contents. Greenough sprang to his feet and began walking restlessly about the room; at length, he picked up a rag from the table, a palette from its nail on the wall, paused in front of a shelf, and stood staring vaguely at a row of bottles.

"Are you looking for something?" Pierce asked.

"My bottle of paint remover. I can't think what's become of it."

"You'll find it on some cliff top, no doubt."

Greenough laughed. "I never use it out of doors. I want to clean this palette. The bottle ought to be right here on the shelf."

"What sort of bottle?"

"Black glass. One of those squat bottles that liqueurs come in; this had a seal. It must have been Benedictine. The can leaked, and I got an empty bottle from Bella."

"Where had she found it?"

"How should I know? Wait a minute – I remember now, I met Bella coming out of Marie's room. She must have been helping with the cleaning for she was carrying a dustpan of rubbish, and I saw that bottle and asked for it and..."

"A bottle from Marie's room?" Pierce sat erect. "A liqueur bottle! Good God, do you see what this means, Greenough? Remember the remark you overheard 'I shall enjoy it extremely.' Liqueur! Strong tasting, with a heavy aroma she would never suspect it had been doped. We're getting somewhere at last!"

"You're right!" Greenough exclaimed. "That is, if the bottle really was found in Marie's room the morning after her death – Bella would know, of course."

"Unluckily, Bella is still *incommunicado*. Can't you fix the date?"

"Let's see. I finished my second Pueblo picture that week, and I remember I was stretching another canvas when I found the paint remover leaked. So it was a cloudy day – if it had been bright I would have been out working on my Rancho picture. And we've had only one grey day for ever so long. Yes!" Greenough drew a long breath. "I can fix the day – It *was* the day after Marie died."

They stared at each other for a moment in silence. Then Pierce said slowly "And the liqueur bottle has vanished. Do you realize that all this takes us straight back to the stool accident? You had seen. You had heard. You must be got rid of. Now, who could have known that when you were painting on the cliff top you would sit at that exact spot?"

"Lots of people. I have shown my picture to most of the guests here at the hotel, and I may have described the ledge and how close it was to the rim. And of course all the painters would know, for it's the only place you can get a bird's eye view of the Pueblo. When the child at the motor camp spoke of a man climbing up the cliff path, I thought it might be Magilp or even Julia Joy. She wears slacks and a corduroy coat. But it's fantastic to suspect either of them!"

"It is. But I'd like to know more about that climber. A family such as you describe couldn't travel fast. On the chance they haven't got farther than Santa Fe, I'm going to call up some friends of mine there and ask them to make a round of cheap tourist camps in the neighbourhood, and, if the child is found, try what they can do with candy and conversation. Not that I am hoping to involve any of your painter friends, Greenough. I am eliminating them from our list of enemies, because of the stolen liqueur bottle, if it was stolen. Mightn't it have been broken by a careless maid and taken away?"

"Not without my knowledge. Paint remover has a horrible smell."

"All right. It was stolen. After the cliff top attempt on your life had failed, because it was the only tangible bit of evidence and might have been traced, and it must have been stolen by someone who knew his, or her, way about the hotel. In short, by a servant or a guest."

"The same servant or guest that I overheard talking to Marie?"

"Of course. Well, I must be going." Pierce rose. "Our talk has answered a lot of questions. Marie Leclair did not die a natural death. Her murder is directly connected with the murder of Mrs Kearny-Pine. The murderer suspected you of knowing too much and an attempt was made to get rid of you. The liqueur bottle must have been stolen by some guest or servant. If you can dig up a few more clues as valuable as these, my work here will be at an end."

This conversation had taken a good deal longer than Pierce had expected. To his satisfaction, he found Garcia's store not yet overrun with tourists and he could be waited upon by Mr Garcia himself. Mr Garcia produced a tray of knives varying from bowie knives of the most ferocious description to tiny silver trinkets encrusted with turquoise and abalone shell.

"You haven't a very large assortment. Have you sold many hunting knives during the last few days?" Pierce ventured.

"Why, there was a lady from the hotel bought one a few days ago," Mr Garcia said. "And yesterday forenoon a party touring the States took a couple. They came from Quebec. I tell you Tecos is…"

"I'll have this one please," Pierce picked up a knife at random, and Mr Garcia proceeded to wrap it up. "You say you sold a hunting knife to a lady from the hotel? That must have been one of the Miss Burleighs."

"No, it wasn't them. I don't know the name of this one, though I've seen her around. She said she wanted it for a boy at the Pueblo."

"At the Pueblo?"

"Yeh. Seems she tied up a cut finger or something and took a fancy to the boy."

"I see." Pierce bade Mr Garcia good-bye and went on his way in a very thoughtful frame of mind.

A visit to Doctor Sylvestro came next on Pierce's list. The doctor might be able to add some information about Marie's death. He found the house, an adobe in a dingy crooked back alley. The door was opened by the doctor in person, and Pierce, with manly welcoming bows and smiles, was ushered into a dark little room and seated in the least dilapidated chair.

"What can I do for you, sir?" the little man beamed. "It is Mr Pierce, I believe?"

Pierce explained his purpose in coming, but the doctor shook his head sadly. No, he had seen nothing, heard nothing that was in any way suspicious. He had of course made inquiries.

Pierce thanked the doctor and rose, scrutiny of his face having convinced him that if the little man knew anything it would not be let out. "By the way," he remarked, picking up his hat, "as a matter of routine, the police want to check up the medicines that Mrs Kearny-Pine was in the habit of using. Did you by any chance preserve the bottle of sedative found in the maid's room after her death? I understand you were called in."

Doctor Sylvestro stared, but he answered readily enough "I believe I did bring it home, and if it has not been thrown away – I never use that preparation – it is at your disposal." He opened a cupboard, and ran his eye up and down the dusty shelves. "Yes, here it is." He handed Pierce a small squar-ish blue bottle, labelled Somnola.

"Thanks," Pierce nodded. "I'll take it along."

Mr Bush the druggist was standing in his doorway. Pierce stopped. They exchanged greetings.

"Do you keep a patent medicine called Somnola?" Pierce asked.

"Why, yes, Mr Pierce, I do. But I can't sell you any without you having a doctor's prescription. It's got morphine in it."

"I don't want to buy any. I only want to see what the bottle looks like."

"That's easy."

In a moment, a bottle, twin to the one in Pierce's pocket, was before him. "Thanks," he handed it back. "How many tablets come in a bottle, and what's the usual dose?"

"There's fifty in a bottle. Folks most commonly take one tablet, and another if the first don't work."

"How many would be fatal?"

"Couldn't say. But I don't guess four would hurt any, 'thout you was more'n common susceptible."

"Thanks." Pierce returned to the hotel, and went straight up to his room. He uncorked the bottle, took out a plug of cotton, emptied the tablets into a pin-tray on the dressing table and counted them. There were forty-six.

"So Marie took only four at the most," he mused, "and she was stout and red-faced and strong as a horse. That settles it. The person Greenough overheard in Marie's room gave her a bottle of liqueur dosed with morphine, intended to stupefy – so the pearls could be stolen – but not to kill. Marie took her usual sedative before going to bed, and the double dose proved fatal. Yes, I was right."

He left the room, walked down the passageway to Greenough's door and would have knocked, but it stood ajar.

"If you leave your door open like this," he remarked as he entered, "Marie's liqueur bottle could have been stolen without much difficulty. I suppose you lock up when you go off for the day?"

"I never lock my door," Greenough said, looking up from the palette he was scraping with a bit of glass. "It never occurred to me there was anything here worth stealing. How have you been getting on this morning? Any more clues?"

"I picked up a fragment or two, I'll discuss them with you as soon as I have had time to put them together. What I came in for, was to find out whether you spoke of your cliff top adventure when you came home that day. Did anyone know about it?"

"No, we kept it to ourselves."

"Good! I'm thankful you didn't discuss it, for a very good reason which you don't seem to have thought of, Greenough. Your enemy does not know that his trap has been sprung. And until he finds that out, he isn't likely to make another attempt on your life."

"Good God! Do you really think..."

"Of course I do," Pierce said impatiently. "I wish you'd get it through your head that there's a killer at large right here in the hotel! So far as I can see, you aren't in any danger at present for the murderer is still hoping for news of a convenient accident – but you've got to watch your step. I want you to promise me you'll keep your door locked, even in the daytime and whether you are in or out, and at night you must not only bolt it but prop a heavy chair against the knob."

"All right. I promise."

"Good." Pierce turned to go, and paused. "It's a heavenly day," he remarked. "Why don't you take Rosalie for a drive after lunch and ask Miss Gryce to go along?"

Greenough was, of course, more than willing to oblige. Within a couple of hours, Pierce was free to embark on the search he had in mind.

Rather to his surprise he found Miss Gryce's bedroom door unlocked. He went in and bolted the door to prevent the chambermaid coming in with her pass key, which wasn't likely as the bed had already been made. Everything in the room was remarkably neat. On the desk was a red leather portfolio stamped with the initials J. G. in gold. Inside it he found writing paper, stamps, three harmless communications from New York stores, a note from a Mrs Baird, and two papers which proved to be, as he had hoped, a nurse's certificates from the T. and C. Hospital.

The names, he saw at once, without the aid of a microscope, had been altered from the original Jane Greer to Janet Gryce, for the ink differed in colour, though so little that only a trained eye would have observed it. The note from Miss Baird, stamped By-the-Bay, Cold Spring Harbour, Long Island, proved to be a recommendation. Here it too was plain that the name Janet Gryce had formerly been Jane Greer.

He left the room, undecided whether or not to give these two new clues to the police. He finally decided to wait until after the inquest and allow Miss Gryce to give her evidence before an unprejudiced audience.

16

The inquest came off next day. As Pierce was leaving the hotel for Garcia's store, he was joined by Greenough, eager to know whether Pierce's Santa Fe friends had succeeded in finding the motor camp child and extracting any valuable information.

"They found him all right. But nothing came of it," Pierce sighed. "All he could add to what he told you was 'something green'."

"Something green? The climber was wearing a green coat or hat?"

"Probably. And green garments are too common to tell us anything much. It's a disappointment. Another much more serious disappointment is Mr Carboy's failure to get here in time for the inquest."

An outside staircase, steep and narrow, took them up into a large bare dusty room. It was hot, sun poured in through unshaded windows.

Rows of small hard chairs for the spectators filled half the space.

At the farther end, various officials were grouped around a table. Near them, at one side, a row of chairs accommodated the jury, at the other, a chair had been placed for witnesses.

Greenough moved forward and sat down beside Rosalie. Pierce took a seat as near to the jury as he could get, and glanced about with some disfavour.

However, the proceedings started well, and went on so smoothly that Pierce was beginning to feel his anxiety had been slightly absurd, when an unexpected bit of testimony upset Stephen Pine's apple cart with a vengeance.

It was not Steve's fault. He had made an unexpectedly good

impression. Pierce had warned him that irritability or unwillingness to answer questions would only prolong his ordeal. Steve had kept his temper, and the grand manner that he could assume if he chose had impressed the coroner.

Rosalie Colbrook's testimony had accomplished even more than Pierce had hoped. It was brief, for Pierce had cautioned her not to volunteer anything, and the coroner was kind.

Miss Gryce had appeared equally well in her own way. She was composed, straightforward and gave an impression of rectitude throughout.

The coroner began by asking for the details of her engagement by the deceased. She then went on to describe Mrs Kearny-Pine's physical condition prior to her death in language that was not too technical to be understood by the jury.

When Mr Atwater was inquired for, Pierce produced a telegram from that young man, expressing horror at the terrible news which he had just heard and announcing his immediate return to Tecos. Mrs Couch's testimony, Bustard's and Pierce's own, were merely routine. Nor did Miller, the hotel clerk, or the hotel servants, reveal anything of interest.

Then Pedro was called. The coroner bade him describe the events of the fatal morning in detail. Pedro told a straightforward story.

A few minutes before eleven the bell in the living room had rung; he had answered it and found Mrs Kearny-Pine sitting on the sofa, embroidering. She had asked him to open one of the windows. He had done so and had turned to go, leaving the door wide open. She had called him back and told him to close the door part way; he had done so and departed. He had never seen her again... alive. After that he had gone to his dinner and did not return to the hall until a few minutes past twelve. During this interval the hall was probably empty, for this was the least busy hour of the day. Mr Miller usually went to his room for a nap. Lost Arrow ought to have been somewhere about, but as he would have been out on the sidewalk, he would have seen nothing that went on inside the hotel.

After dinner, Pedro continued, he had gone on an errand. When he returned to the hotel he saw Mr Atwater in the doorway, looking out. When Pedro came up, Mr Atwater pushed past him without speaking and hurried away down the street.

"What's that?" the coroner broke in. "You say that Mr Algernon Atwater, nephew of the deceased, was present in the hall of the hotel a few minutes after twelve o'clock on the morning of Tuesday last! That has not been mentioned before."

Pedro explained: he had forgotten to speak of having seen Mr Atwater that day, because it did not seem important. But when the coroner had told him to go over every minute of that particular hour he had remembered seeing Mr Atwater.

The coroner reflected for a moment, and a whisper ran through the audience. Then he said: "No doubt Mr Atwater can explain his visit to the hotel when he arrives. You may go on, Pedro."

Pedro had nothing more to tell of any interest until he came to the discovery of the body in the living room. Here Bustard leaned forward and whispered to the coroner; the coroner nodded.

"Did you hear any of the persons who were present when the body was found make any remark that attracted your attention, Pedro?" the coroner asked.

Pedro thought for a moment, and shook his head. "Mrs Couch screamed, and I heard Miss Colbrook crying as if her heart would break. But I don't remember hearing anybody say anything. We just stood looking at the body without saying a word till Mr Pine came in."

"And did Mr Pine say anything? How did he behave?"

"Mr Pine? Why he just took one look and then he stepped back like he'd been shot and he said: 'Lulu – poor little Lulu. Forgive me. I didn't mean to do it.' And then he sort of choked up and hid his face in his two hands and cried."

There was a moment's dead silence. Then the coroner said: "If that is all, Pedro, you may sit down," and turned to Bustard. They conferred for a moment, then the coroner said apologetically: "Mr Pine, I must ask you to return." Steve stood up. He was looking red and angry but not, Pierce observed, in the least alarmed.

"Will you tell the jury what you meant by the remark the last witness has alluded to, Mr Pine?"

Steve frowned. "I didn't quite get what the fellow says I said."

"According to Pedro Diaz," the coroner said, "when you caught sight of the body of your deceased wife, you exclaimed: 'Lulu – poor little Lulu. Forgive me. I didn't mean to do it.' "

"Did I say that? I don't remember what I said. I was too horrified to know what I was saying."

"But suppose those were your words," the coroner persisted, "how would you explain their meaning?"

"I must have meant I was sorry," Steve said confusedly. "Sorry for not having paid any attention to her when she said she was frightened – and – other things..."

"Frightened?" the coroner asked.

But before he could go on, Rosalie sprang to her feet. "Oh, please," she exclaimed, "I did not tell you about Cousin Louisa's being frightened! May I tell you now?"

Everyone listened with intense interest as she described the visit to Governor Dane's house and Mrs Kearny-Pine's subsequent unaccountable alarm. When she sat down there was a satisfied nodding of heads in the audience.

Soon after, the inquest came to an end with the expected verdict of "wilful murder by some person or persons unknown."

Pierce left the room very low in his mind. For one thing, he was mortified at having neglected to talk over with Pedro the scene in the living room after the discovery of the body. He had been too far away from Steve on that occasion to catch more than "Lulu – poor little Lulu," and had missed the concluding words. There was Algy Atwater, too, messing everything up! Why had Pedro never spoken of meeting Algy coming out of the hotel that morning? Pierce knew that none of the family would be allowed to leave Tecos for New York the next day. The private car waiting for them at Lamy would have to be countermanded.

Absorbed in these gloomy reflections, Pierce did not speak as he walked back to the hotel with Steve, who was equally silent until, as they went in, he took Pierce's arm. "Come upstairs with me, Hubert," he said quietly. "I want to talk to you."

Together they went on to a room on the second floor which Mrs Couch had tactfully provided as a sitting room for the family. Steve said "I wish you would repeat those words that the coroner seemed to think so important. I can't for the life of me remember just what I said when I saw Louisa dead."

"All I heard was, 'Lulu – poor little Lulu.' But according to Pedro, you went on 'Forgive me, I didn't mean to do it!' "

"That couldn't have been it exactly," Steve said, considering. "I think I said: 'I didn't mean it!' "

"Not quite the same thing," Pierce agreed, "and Pedro might easily have got it wrong. But if it was that, Steve, just what was in your mind?"

"Why, only that I was sorry for - for a lot of things. Partly, as I told the coroner, I was sorry that I hadn't paid any attention to Louisa when she told me she had been frightened about something. But another thing I was a lot more sorry for – and what I meant about 'not meaning it' – was having told Louisa, when I first got here the other day, that I wanted a divorce."

"A divorce! Have you spoken to anyone else about wanting a divorce?"

Steve flushed. "Well, only to the – the lady. I – I ..."

"I see." Arabella! Pierce said to himself. "How do you feel about it now?"

"Rotten," Steve muttered, looking at the floor. "You know Louisa and I didn't hit it off any too well. But when I saw here there – like that – it come back to me how she looked when we first met. Louisa wasn't ever what you'd call handsome, but she had a nice colour and pretty hair – and she was awfully in love with me – God!" he ended. "If I could get her back, I'd let her nag me and take me to church till all was blue."

Pierce said nothing for a few minutes. "It's an unfortunate combination of circumstances," he began, and broke off. There was a knock at the door. Pedro came in with a note for Steve, and departed.

Steve read it with a puzzled frown. Pierce had guessed the contents. He was not surprised when Steve exclaimed indignantly:

"This is the limit! The district attorney wants us to stay in Tecos until Algy gets here! Now why in hell is that necessary?"

Before Pierce could answer, Rosalie came in. "Thank goodness that horrible inquest is over," she said as she perched herself on the arm of Steve's chair. "When do we leave tomorrow? Right after breakfast, I suppose? What a relief it will be to get away!"

"We can't go home tomorrow after all," Steve said dully. "The district attorney wants us to wait until Algy gets back, and it seems that what he says goes, according to Hubert."

"Until Algy gets back? But that won't be until tomorrow night!" Rosalie cried. "Why under the sun should we stay for Algy?"

"God knows why!" Steve shrugged his shoulders, rose heavily and left the room.

"Poor Cousin Steve," Rosalie murmured, and turned to Pierce. "Why does the district attorney want us to stay until Algy gets here?" she demanded. "And why do we have to do what he tells us to?"

"Just a matter of routine. Lawyers are apt to be obstructionists, you know. The legal mind can busy itself with red tape to a quite extraordinary extent."

"I see." But Rosalie looked far from satisfied, and Pierce was relieved when Pedro appeared again, announcing the arrival of Mr Carboy and party; Mr Pierce was wanted downstairs at once.

The party was large and imposing. The vice president of the Golden Chain was here. So were the managers of the New York and Chicago branches. Miller was assigning rooms and distributing keys, Manuel and Pedro collecting hand luggage. The more important members of the group were introduced, then Carboy asked Pierce where they could talk, and the two took refuge in the writing room.

"I thought we'd never get here," Carboy groaned as he sank into a chair. "It's been an infernal journey. One delay after another."

"You ought to have flown, as I did."

"I know, I know! Don't rub it in. I'll never forgive myself for arriving too late for the inquest. How did it go? Begin at the beginning and tell me all about everything."

Pierce obeyed. When he had finished, Carboy sat silent for a long moment. Then:

"A strange affair," he said slowly. "I don't understand it. Is there something back of it all, Pierce?"

"Perhaps. But what? An enemy? Blackmail?"

"Not blackmail. She was too strong minded to submit to that sort of thing. She had plenty of enemies, of course. When Peerless went down, thousands of stockholders must have cursed the Golden Chain. She was well hated, Pierce."

"Can you suggest any motive except robbery?"

"No. No. It must have been robbery. And I agree with your theory there is a connection between Mrs Kearny-Pine's murder and the death of the maid. You have investigated the past of everyone who was in the hotel at that time, of course?"

"Pretty well. They are all rich and all highly respectable. With one exception, a shabby little parson named Wurtz. If he had turned out to be that clerical crook the Bishop was after – but I heard just now that the Bishop's man has been caught. What's more, I don't think Wurtz has the necessary mentality. And, for various reasons I needn't go into now, I am inclined to eliminate the trained nurse. We seem to be up against a blank wall."

"We certainly are, I only wish the district attorney were equally puzzled. You think he has fixed on Stephen Pine?"

"I think so. And the case against Steve is better than anything I have to offer."

Dinner over, most of the travellers from New York, tired out, went straight to their rooms. When Mr Carboy and Pierce came out of the dining room they found a rather oddly assorted group gathered around the hall fire, the district attorney, the coroner, Bustard, John Greenough, Mrs Couch and a couple of reporters. They were talking cheerfully and seemed in excellent spirits. Even Mrs Couch was able to draw a long breath and begin planning for the future.

That future certainly needed planning. Most of her guests had gone. John Greenough, of course, remained; and Professor Bridges was staying on – he was on the track of a rare flower James Rio had told him about. As for Mr Wurtz, Mrs Couch sincerely wished that he also would take his departure. Miss Spingle, the school teacher from Kansas City on a sabbatical, would be leaving tomorrow. All the others guests – Plummers, Burleighs and what not – had drifted away like leaves before an autumn wind. But Mrs Couch was not quite as depressed as she might have been. Mr Pine had promised to make it all right as far as her vacant rooms were concerned, and the sad events of the past few days had undoubtedly put Tecos on the map.

When Pierce and Mr Carboy joined the group, Connor, the district attorney, was describing various murder trials in which he had taken part, and discussing crime in general.

"The motive is the thing," he said.

"The motive is a very important factor," Pierce agreed. "But to my mind, character is almost equally so."

The district attorney snorted contemptuously. "Character? I don't take much stock in character. In my experience, *anybody* is capable of *anything*. And I believe there are only two basic motives for crime: love and money. Every crime I ever handled could be traced back to either love or money. Or to those two turned wrong side out."

"Love, money and revenge are the classic motives for crime," Pierce said. "And revenge is out of fashion. We moderns..." He paused, as a low voice broke in:

"Mr Connor, may I speak to you for a moment?"

It was James Rio. Connor rose at once. As the two went off to the writing room, Professor Bridges joined the group around the fire. His clothes were dusty and he seemed tired. He said he had ridden more than thirty mile in search of the orchid James Rio had told him about without finding a trace of it, not even a sprout. He inquired rather perfunctorily about the inquest, and was listening to Bustard's account, when the district attorney and James Rio came back. Connor said:

"Have a cigar, James. What's your hurry? Sit down and have a smoke."

James Rio accepted the cigar with a bow and sat down a little in the background, upright and dignified.

"To go back to the subject of discussion," one of the reporters remarked. "You don't think revenge a likely motive for murder nowadays?"

"Not with people like you and me," Connor grinned. "We think too much of our own skins. If we hanker for revenge we ask the law to give it to us."

"What would you say to that, James Rio?" Bustard asked. "Do you know anybody who would kill for the sake of getting even? For revenge?"

James Rio took the cigar out of his mouth and regarded the sheriff for a moment before he answered, speaking with extreme deliberation, "Revenge? That is still a very great reason for murder – Love... Money... Revenge..." He nodded solemnly. "All three are good reasons for killing. My people kill for all those reasons."

17

The evening's conversation had given Pierce food for thought. Evidently Connor and Bustard were involved in an important irrigation project that depended on the Pueblo and James Rio for success. Pierce went slowly upstairs; as he was passing Janet Gryce's room on the way to his own, she stepped out.

"I've been waiting to speak to you, Mr Pierce," she whispered. "I couldn't go to sleep because of worrying about Mr Pine – what he said when he saw the body."

"I wouldn't worry about that, Miss Gryce," Pierce said impatiently. "It's not important."

"Not important! Why, it seemed to me that Mr Connor thought that remark of Mr Pine's very important. Oh, Mr Pierce – you – don't suppose Mr Pine could – could have done it!"

"Certainly not," Pierce said angrily. "What put such an absurd idea into your head?"

"Seems absurd to me too, but," she lowered her voice to a horrified whisper, "I keep remembering that he was called 'Tiger' at college."

"Who said so?" Pierce demanded.

"Miss Clara Burleigh. Their cousin was at Princeton with Mr Pine, and just before the Burleighs left the hotel they got talking about him, and Miss Clara said he'd got into some awful scrape at college – nearly killed a caddie or something – and was suspended. Miss Clara said everybody knew that Stephen Pine had an ungovernable temper and that his wife's friends were awfully worried when she insisted on marrying him, although she was ten years older than he was, and that he only wanted her money. Oh, Mr Pierce, wouldn't it be terrible if the district attorney heard all that!"

"Look here, Miss Gryce," Pierce spoke sternly. "It isn't up to you either to defend or accuse Mr Pine. But we can't talk here. May I come into your room?" She nodded.

"You don't suppose that Mr Pine is in any danger of being arrested?" she continued, "that the reason the district attorney won't let the family leave Tecos is because be suspects Mr Pine?"

"Certainly not. As a matter of fact, Miss Gryce, you yourself are the only person I know of who is in any danger of arrest!"

"What!" she cried, and fell back into a chair as if he had struck her. "I? I? Why, I wouldn't have hurt a hair of her head – she was my patient!"

Pierce felt the ring of sincerity in her cry of horror, although another communication from the Society for the Nourishment of Infant Paupers had made it abundantly plain that she really was Jane Greer and that Jane Greer was a thief.

"Why? Why?" she panted, pale and wild eyed. "Why should I be suspected?"

"Because of your past. I know your story. I know that your real name is Jane Greer and that you changed it because you were trying to escape from justice. You are wanted by the New York police for stealing a considerable sum of money from the charitable society you have been working with for the past year."

She stared at him silently, wonder seeming to overwhelm her fear. "How did you find out?" she gasped.

"Never mind how I know. It's enough that I do know. What, in heaven's name, induced you to get mixed up in a thing like that, Miss Gryce? You look like such a nice girl."

"You'll never believe me if I tell you. No man could. I did it because I wanted money to buy pretty clothes."

"Clothes!"

"Yes, clothes. You see, the man I was engaged to began going with another girl and I thought it was partly because she always looked so smart. And I was awfully in love... And the 'Infant Paupers' aren't any too liberal when it comes to salaries..."

"I see," Pierce sighed. "I gather that you faked cases and kept back part of the money entrusted to you for relief?"

"It sounds terrible when you put it like that," she faltered. "But it didn't hurt the children any. I did my best for all the *real* poor children I was taking care of... I only stole from the ones that didn't exist," she explained, and the shadow of a smile curled her lips. "It's awful to say so, but in the beginning it was sort of fun."

"Fun?"

"Fun fooling the superintendent, who thinks such a lot of herself, and all those solemn lady managers that don't know beans about poor children, and every one of 'em rich as Crocus. A pack of geese. Seemed like they'd swallow anything. And that was where I made my mistake," she ended ruefully. "I got careless. Asked for spectacles for crippled children, or braces for the myopic – something silly like that."

"I see." Pierce suppressed a smile. "Now, to go back to what we were saying about your being suspected –"

Again, terror swept all other emotion from her face, and he went on more gently: "Don't look so despairing. I may not be obliged to give you away."

"How do you mean?"

"Merely that the district attorney may never think of examining your record and I may not need to attract his attention to it. Mr Pine is my client and my first duty is to him. If Connor decides that he has a good enough case to warrant his holding Mr Pine for the Grand Jury, I shall do my utmost to prevent it. For I am convinced that Mr Pine had nothing whatever to do with the murder of his wife. I hope to induce the district attorney to share my opinion. But if I do not succeed I may be forced to suggest the possibility of some other person being the guilty party."

"You mean me?" she whispered.

Pierce nodded.

"Do you really mean that if Mr Connor decides that Mr Pine is guilty you will tell him what you know about me? But is that fair?

If you think I did that terrible thing you ought to tell him anyway."

"Not as I see it. For one thing, I'm not at all sure that you did kill her." He smiled as she drew a long breath of relief. "But your record, and the fact that you suppressed letters addressed to your employer that were injurious to yourself, will make things look bad for you. I could use you as a red herring, Miss Gryce. Don't get too downhearted," he went on. "Any minute something may develop that will take Mr Pine and his family out of the limelight and turn the investigation into a safer direction for you. But you'd better keep that gossip about Mr Pine's college career to yourself. For the moment, your safety hinges on his." And with this word of advice he left her.

But the interview had confirmed a previous impression, Janet Gryce was not the type to commit murder. He decided to wait. I can't help liking the girl, he said to himself, as he went to his room. If we ever get through this muddle I'll make Steve give her that pitiful four hundred dollars she stole and send her back to the 'Infant Paupers' to confess and pay up.

The next day seemed long to most of the persons concerned in the Kearny-Pine murder case. The district attorney, the sheriff, Pierce, Mr Carboy and the reporters were all marking time, waiting for Algy Atwater's return to Tecos, which could not be earlier than nine o'clock that night.

Hubert Pierce decided to while away the morning at the Pueblo. He wanted to ask about the knife Janet Gryce was reported to have given to an Indian boy, and also test her veracity in the matter of moccasins.

He found the Pueblo returned to everyday life, though still limp and exhausted from the long long obsequies for Wind-from-the-Mountain. James Rio greeted him politely and showed him around in his usual dignified manner, ending with the gallery of paintings, when a little boy joined them.

"Your son?" Pierce asked. "A fine little fellow. What is his name?"

"My youngest son," James Rio smiled proudly. "Indian name, Little Poplar Tree. American name, Peter."

"This must be the little chap who cut his hand the other day," Pierce remarked. "A lady at the Blue Santo Hotel, Miss Gryce, told me about his accident."

"The lady made my hand well. She gave me this knife," the boy said proudly, and he drew a hunting knife from a leather sheath that hung at his belt.

Pierce congratulated James Rio on the boy, verified Janet's statement that her moccasins had been a present and took his leave, more than ever convinced that her criminal career had begun and ended in New York.

There were, however, two persons concerned in the murder case who did not find the morning long: Rosalie Colbrook and John Greenough. They had started out directly after breakfast in Greenough's car, returning to the hotel very late for lunch, engaged to be married and in a dazed condition that made them unconscious of hunger or fatigue and oblivious of everything in heaven and earth but their two selves.

After dinner much the same group gathered around the hall fire as on the previous night. The case was not directly discussed but a knowing glance that went from Bustard to Connor when Miss Clara Burleigh happened to be mentioned, convinced Pierce that Bustard had interviewed that lady before her departure and had learned, from her, Stephen Pine's unfortunate nickname.

At a little before nine o'clock, James Rio came in and had another interview with the district attorney and Bustard in the writing room. They both appeared so annoyed when they returned to the hall that Pierce guessed James Rio had reported the Pueblo in a mood unfavourable to irrigation schemes. James Rio was presented with a cigar, accepted it with dignity, and had seated himself when a motor horn sounded outside. Everyone started, and every head was turned, as Pedro opened the front door and ushered in a young man, white faced and rather dishevelled as to dress.

The district attorney stepped forward. "Mr Algernon Atwater, I presume?" he said. "I am Mr Connor."

Algy stared, as if wondering why the devil he was being given this bit of information, and turned to Pedro, who carried a large pigskin bag. "Where is Mr Pine?" he demanded. "Upstairs? Then I'll go right up."

"Mr Atwater," Connor interposed, "I am the district attorney. I must have a word with you at once. As soon as you have greeted your family, will you be so good as to return here? We can talk in the writing room."

Algy nodded carelessly and went upstairs two steps at a time. After an interval of some twenty minutes, he returned with Stephen Pine.

He had evidently brushed up, and looked less fatigued as he approached the fire and gave the district attorney an off-hand nod.

"You want to talk to me, Mr Connor?" he remarked "Well, here I am. Fire away. Not that I can tell you anything. You might as well ask the man in the moon who could have committed this beastly crime. Of course, it was some fellow who wanted the pearls."

Without speaking, the district attorney led the way into the writing room, followed by Algy and Stephen, Bustard, Pierce and Mr Carboy. The door was shut.

They all sat down and Connor began with routine questions, which Algy answered with a nonchalant, not to say insolent, indifference, making it clear that he considered Connor a rather absurd person but was willing to humour him, until the latter said:

"Now, Mr Atwater, will you please tell us when you last saw your aunt, Mrs Kearny-Pine?"

The fat white hand twiddling a lock of hair dropped to Algy's knee. There was hesitation in his answer:

"I don't quite remember. Two or three days before her death."

"Then you did not see your aunt on the morning of Tuesday last? The morning of the murder?"

"No, I did not."

"But you came here to the hotel that morning?"

There was a perceptible pause before the answer: "Yes; I did come to the hotel that morning, but I did not see my aunt."

"What was the object of your visit?"

"You want to know why I called on my aunt?" Algy raised his eyebrows. "That's an impertinent question. I came on private business."

"Private business?" Connor gave Algy a satisfied smile. "Well, we'll let it go at that – for the moment. You say you did not see your aunt, Mrs Kearny-Pine, on the morning in question?"

"I did not. As I have already said, I came here to the hotel to call on my aunt. l waited for a few minutes in the hall and then I changed my mind. I decided to come again some other time and went home."

"You changed your mind? And the reason for your changing your mind with such startling suddenness is connected with this private business which you do not wish to discuss?"

Algy only shrugged his shoulders, and Connor went on: "Mr Atwater, I must insist on knowing your reason for leaving the hotel so suddenly without seeing your aunt."

Algy was silent for a moment. Then: "I funked it," he said sulkily.

"So you expected the interview with your aunt would be of a disagreeable nature!" Connor snapped. "Had you quarrelled with the lady?"

For the first time, Algy seemed really disturbed. Connor and Bustard exchanged glances. "What of it?" he muttered. "My aunt and I didn't always agree, of course. But I can't see what business it is of yours."

The district attorney leaned forward and rapped the table with his pencil. "See here, Mr Atwater – I've had about enough of this back talk from you. Listen to me! Mrs Kearny-Pine is known to have been murdered between eleven and twelve o'clock on Tuesday last. At about five minutes past twelve you were seen here in the hotel, but hurried away as soon as you were observed. You hurried around to the garage, hired a car and went to your studio, where you hurriedly packed a travelling bag and drove away with every appearance of haste. In fact, you were so expeditious, that within *half an hour* of the time you were seen here in the hotel, you were on your way to the junction where you took the train to Los Angeles and you have the face to tell me that all this – your presence on the spot at the time the murder was committed and your abrupt departure immediately afterwards, your having quarrelled with your aunt as you yourself admit – that all this is none of my business?"

"I have nothing to say," Algy muttered. "You are just trying to trip me up. Mr Carboy is a lawyer; you can talk to him."

"Very well. Then you and Mr Pine will please withdraw." Connor indicated chairs at the farther side of the room. "You, too, Mr Carboy and Mr Pierce, while Bustard and I talk things over."

The four men did as they were told. The district attorney and Bustard, their heads close together, began a discussion that threatened to last some time. They spoke in whispers, but Pierce caught a word now and then, and as their glances rested now on Algy and now on Stephen, he realized they were not arguing about Algy – they knew Algy could be held for the Grand Jury, but were debating Stephen Pine's guilt. Was Pine implicated? Had he instigated the crime and made Algy his tool?

This was worse than Pierce had feared. He cursed Algy Atwater for a fool – if Algy had kept a civil tongue in his head and not got Connor's s back up, the thing might have been staved off for a while. And he fumbled in his pocket for the message from the Society for the Nourishment of Infant Paupers which, when it was presented to the district attorney, would bring Janet Gryce into the case and at least confuse the issue.

After some ten minutes discussion, the district attorney looked up.

"Mr Pine and Mr Atwater," he said solemnly, "please step forward."

They did so. "It is with great regret," Connor went on, "that I find it my duty to hold you both for the Grand Jury. I ..."

"Mr Connor," Pierce broke in. He rose and approached the table. "Excuse me for interrupting you. But I have here a most important communication. I wish you would read this telegram before you..."

He stopped. Every head turned, for a peremptory knock had sounded on the door.

18

In the meantime the group around the hall fire, waiting to hear the outcome of Algy Atwater's examination by the district attorney, had been augmented by the arrival of Professor Bridges, who came in looking even dustier and more fatigued than on the previous evening. But he unstrapped the vasculum from his shoulder with an air of triumph and Greenough, who admired the little man's adventurous spirit, exclaimed: "You look so pleased I'm sure you must have found your orchid!"

"Yes, I found it." Professor Bridges slipped the catch of the tin case, disclosed a tangle of damp moss, took out a spray of flowers, shaped like butterflies, clear bright turquoise blue in tint, the tips of the petals streaked with deeper colour, and held it out for admiration, regarding it with his head on one side like a hen surveying an unusually fine egg.

"Isn't it lovely!" Mrs Couch said. "I've never seen one like that before."

"I found it on the cliff where James Rio told me to look." The professor gave him a grateful nod. "As I hoped, but as I scarcely dared to expect, it is an orchid, a new species of *Serapias*. Moreover, it is, as you see, blue and a blue orchid is as rare as a blue poppy. It will, of course, be named after me *Serapias Bridgesi*. My colleagues will be exceedingly envious."

As he replaced the flower tenderly in the case, John Greenough, who knew the professor's methodical habits, asked: "Aren't you going to put it in water?"

"No," the professor sighed. "No, I have other, even more important matters that must first be attended to. Where is the district attorney?"

"In the writing room," several voices answered at once and

every eye followed the little man as he turned away, knocked at the door of the writing room and, without waiting for permission, walked in.

"What do you want, Professor?" Connor asked sharply. "I am very busy now, and..."

"Pardon me for intruding," said the professor. "I would not do so without sufficient reason."

He approached the group around the table and glanced from one serious face to the other – at Stephen Pine, Algy Atwater, Pierce, Carboy and Bustard. Then his eyes came back to the district attorney and rested on that annoyed countenance as he went on "Mr Connor, you are the district attorney. It is my duty to inform you that I have discovered the murderer of Mrs Kearny-Pine."

There was a second's dead silence. Then:

"You have?" Connor exclaimed incredulously. "Is it – is it anyone here?"

"Certainly not," Professor Bridges answered with evident surprise. Four of his hearers drew long breaths of relief, and Bustard bit his lip. "But it is a long story and a complicated one. With your permission I will tell it in my own way, or I shall not be able to make it intelligible. May I sit?"

Connor nodded. Professor Bridges seated himself, took off his spectacles, wiped them and put them on again. "As I remarked, it is a long story," he began, speaking with extreme deliberation, "and it commences a very long way back. Back in the time of the Mexican War, in fact."

Bustard grunted and shuffled his feet. The professor gave him the reproving glance suitable for an unruly pupil, and proceeded:

"The Mexican War is ancient history to Easterners, but in New Mexico it has never been forgotten. In Tecos, the names of persons who figured in that war are alluded to as if they had died last week, in much the same tone and almost as frequently as you will hear the names of Roosevelt or Henry Ford. Such names, I mean, as Kit Carson and General Kearny of the Mexican War... Mr Pine, you are not, I believe, in any way related to General Stephen Watts Kearny?"

"No," Stephen Pine showed surprise at the odd question. "No, I am not a relation of General Kearny's."

"Ah, well." The professor shook his head sadly and went on: "The name Kearny is well remembered in Tecos, but in different ways. Some persons remember the General with gratitude, and others with hate. Mr Connor, last evening when James Rio insisted that revenge was a natural motive for murder, you were inclined to disbelieve him."

Connor only nodded vaguely. Everyone was listening intently to the professor's story but no one had the least idea what he was driving at, and he went serenely on:

"Leaving the Mexican War for the moment, my story comes down to the present, to the arrival of Mrs Stephen Kearny-Pine in Tecos some two weeks since. It appears that when she wrote her name in the hotel register, its similarity to that of a local hero – General Stephen Kearny – was remarked by Pedro who commented upon it in the kitchen and then straight away forgot all about it. But one of the waitresses happened to speak of it to the caretaker of Governor Dane's house and discussion at once began as to whether or not Mrs Kearny-Pine was related to General Kearny, the hereditary enemy of the Tecos Indians. But this would also have come to nothing, except for an odd coincidence. It appears that when Mrs Kearny-Pine wrote her name in the register during the visit to Governor Dane's house described by Miss Colbrook, she wrote so hurriedly that a blot obscured it. Only the front part – Mrs Stephen Kearny – could be read, and it was the excited comments of the husband and brother, when they saw the name, that caused the lady's alarm. However, this second arousing of suspicion would also have died a natural death if Mrs Kearny-Pine had not chanced to admire the image of the Blue Santo –"

"The Blue Santo!" Connor broke in impatiently. "That's the name of this hotel. What in hell do you mean, Professor?"

"No interruptions, I beg." The professor raised his hand and Connor subsided. "As I was about to inform you, the Blue Santo is the image in a blue robe, supposed to be that of a statue, which stands on the mantelpiece of the living room here in the hotel – the very room in which the poor lady came to her death, an ancient work of art which Mrs Kearny-Pine endeavoured to purchase from Mrs Couch without success. But Mrs Kearny-Pine was so determined to have it and talked so much about it that everyone in Tecos began talking about it too. When Mrs Couch finally gave in, Mrs Kearny-Pine made no secret of the purchase price – a thousand dollars, an enormous sum in anyone's eyes. And now, gentlemen." The professor paused, took off his spectacles again, wiped them and replaced them on his nose. "The fat was in the fire with a vengeance! For, extraordinary to relate, that image had once been the property of General Stephen Kearny and had been stolen from his headquarters in Santa Fe, a fact known to the Indians and to the Indians alone."

Every one of the listeners bent forward with intenser interest, for now at last Professor Bridges' story showed where it was leading. Connor would have spoken, but again a pedagogical gesture silenced him.

"When the waitress and the caretaker's family put their heads together," the professor went on, "their collective mind drew the natural inference. No one would pay a thousand dollars for an image except for some secret reason. The lady was undoubtedly General Kearny's daughter, come to Tecos for the express purpose of securing the Blue Santo, a sacred relic of her father, precious to all the Kearny family.

"The waitress took the secret to the Pueblo and whispered it in the ear of one person – only one – the news does not appear to have become a matter of common knowledge. This person was the old chief, Wind-from-the-Mountain; Wind-from-the-Mountain, who as a lad, had witnessed from his hiding place the execution of the six Tecos braves condemned to death by General Kearny, one of them his own father and an innocent man. And thus, gentlemen, was the final ingredient added to the devil's broth of suspicion and hatred which had been brewing for over eighty years!"

"Look here, Professor," Bustard broke in. Bustard had been shuffling his feet – blowing his nose and giving other evidences of impatient incredulity for some time past. "Look ahere! We ain't in Hollywood! I never heard such poppycock in all my born days. Old Wind-from-the-Mountain came down to the hotel and murdered Mrs Kearny-Pine because he thought she was the General's daughter? Why, to my certain knowledge, Wind-from-the-Mountain has been as good as bedridden for years!"

"Pardon me," the professor said drily. "I am not aware of having accused Wind-from-the-Mountain of murder."

His annoyance was so apparent, that Pierce put in soothingly:

"Your knowledge of Indian psychology is remarkable, Professor. How did you learn all this?"

"I am a botanist," the professor said modestly, "and the nature lore of the locals is invaluable to me. The Tecos Indians in particular are remarkably sensitive to the beauties of the flora and fauna of the land. But I must not digress, or Mr Bustard will become even more impatient than he is at present. With Mr Bustard's permission..." – Bustard grinned sheepishly – "I will proceed with my narrative which now reaches today. Early this morning I started on horseback for a cliff on the side of Tecos Mountain some seven miles from the Pueblo, where I hoped to find a rare orchid recently described to me by James Rio. The trail was rough and so little used that it was difficult to follow. More than once I was obliged to retrace my steps. It was some hours before I came in sight of the cliff with a cave at its base, whose summit, according to James Rio, was a likely habitat for the plant in question. The face of the cliff was steep and the trail wound around and achieved the summit from the rear. In a few minutes I emerged on the cliff top and, to my intense satisfaction, immediately perceived a fine specimen of *Serapias* – the plant in question – hitherto unknown to me. I had culled it and was packing it in my vasculum when I became aware of a peculiar sound coming from below. I crept to the verge and peered down. There to my astonishment was a woman, an Indian girl, bending over the embers of a fire and sobbing bitterly as she raked them apart. It was the sound of her weeping that had attracted my attention.

"I mounted my horse, descended the trail, made my way to the cave, and found the girl. At my approach she looked up in alarm. I recognised her at once. The girl was Bella, one of the hotel waitresses."

Professor Bridges came to a dramatic pause, and a buzz of questions began, but Connor broke in with a peremptory: "Go ahead, Professor. We seem to be getting somewhere at last!" and with a complacent smile the professor obeyed:

"I reassured the poor girl, soothed her fears, promised to protect her from whatever danger had driven her to this lonely spot. At length her weeping ceased and I persuaded her to confide in me.

"Bella told me of her discovery that a lady staying in the Blue Santo was the daughter of the hereditary enemy of her race; of how she had carried the news to Wind-from-the-Mountain – Bella was his favourite grandchild and she was accustomed to entertaining the old chief with hotel gossip. She told me of the chief's excitement, of his satisfaction when he learned that the daughter of his ancient enemy was within his power, and of his desire for revenge – the general's daughter must pay the penalty of her father's crime! When Bella refused to become an instrument of revenge, the chief threatened the girl with expulsion from the family and with his everlasting curse in this world and in the world to come. The poor creature was so accustomed to unquestioning obedience she consented. Wind-from-the-Mountain proceeded to plot the crime with meticulous care. Every move was thought out. Bella was told exactly what to do and provided with the weapon – strange to say, from beginning to end, no one else seems to have been let into the secret. It was a matter between Wind-from-the-Mountain and his favourite grandchild.

"Tuesday was fixed upon because Bella had an afternoon off. At eleven o'clock she was told by the cook to take a glass of milk to Mrs Kearny-Pine in the living room..." The professor paused, and turned to Pierce. "Mr Pierce, I presume the glass was tested for fingerprints?"

"No. I was too late for that," Pierce answered. "The glass had, of course, been washed when it came back to the kitchen. But, as I knew that Bella had taken the milk to the writing room, I concluded that any prints found on the glass would have been hers, or Mrs Kearny-Pine's, and therefore of little value in any case."

"I see," the professor's smile was very condescending, "it would seem that even an eminent New York detective sometimes underrates the obvious. To return to poor Bella, at a little after eleven she entered the living room, and placed the glass of milk on the table in front of the sofa where Mrs Kearny-Pine was seated busy with her embroidery, her back to the door. Bella retreated to the door, closed it without leaving the room, returned to the sofa on tiptoe – her soft boots soundless on the thick carpet – and standing behind the lady's back, waited unseen with the knife in her hand. In a moment the lady bent forward to take up the glass of milk and Bella struck! The knife penetrated a vital spot. Death was instantaneous."

A choking groan broke from Stephen Pine. As he hid his face in his hands, Professor Bridges gave him a pitying glance and went on in a lower voice:

"Bella laid the body on the floor, wrapped it in the scarf and cushion, leaving the knife in the wound to stem a betraying flow of blood, and was about to conceal the corpse under the sofa, together with the garments which she had previously secured from Mrs Kearny-Pine's bedroom in order to delay discovery, when her eye was caught by the pearls..."

"The pearls!" Connor and Bustard exclaimed simultaneously, and the professor nodded sadly:

"Yes; the pearls. Bella – poor creature – was ignorant of their value. But they were pretty beads, she slipped them into her pocket. The crime completed, she went out of the room, leaving the door open, and returned to the kitchen where her fellow servants were at dinner, told them she was dining at the Pueblo and hurried off with the news to her eagerly waiting grandfather. She found him alone and told him. Wind-from-the-Mountain gave one loud cry and fell back dead!"

"Died of joy," Connor remarked.

"And makes things a lot easier all round," Bustard added.

"My story is nearly done," the professor said. "When her grandfather fell back dead, Bella's scream brought the women rushing in and to the poor girl's horror, she was accused of having fatigued the old man with her chatter and thus been the cause of his death. In the consequent scene of confusion, Bella secured a packet of food and hurried away up the Mountain trail, scarcely knowing what she did or whither she went. At last she reached the cave. Here she sheltered, trying to decide whether to return to the Pueblo, or to endeavour to cross the mountain range, very difficult on foot, and reach a certain distant village where friends would hide her. A few minutes before I found her, while she was throwing a log on the fire, the pearls had slipped from her neck into the very heart of the flames. This seemed the last straw; sobbing bitterly, she raked among the ashes. It was useless, the pearls were gone, reduced to blackened lumps. But in the embers I found – this!"

Professor Bridges laid a small glittering object on the table in front of the district attorney. Everyone bent forward to examine it closely, except Stephen Pine. He gave one sick glance and hid his face again, while the others stared fascinated at the bit of twisted gold set with an uncut emerald surrounded by small diamonds.

"God!" Algy muttered. "It's the clasp – the clasp of Aunt Louisa's pearl necklace!"

Connor picked up the jewel and turned it over in his hand. "You can see where it was melted in the fire," he remarked, and turned to Algy. "Mr Atwater, you recognize this clasp as being the property of the deceased, Mrs Kearny-Pine?"

"Absolutely," Algy answered. "I was with my aunt in Paris five years ago when she bought it from a dealer in antiques; it had belonged to Marie Antoinette and my aunt paid a large sum for it – I forget just how much."

The district attorney nodded and turned to Professor Bridges.

"Well, Professor," he said respectfully, I take off my hat to you. You're the best sleuth of the lot. What happened next? We got to get that girl, you know. Finish your story."

"There is little more to tell." The professor's manner was slightly apologetic. "I gave Bella my horse and the little money and food I had about me, and walked home."

"Good God! You let her go?" Connor exclaimed incredulously. "And she's had several hours start of us. If she managed to reach another pueblo we might as well hunt for a needle in a haystack. Where did you say she was bound for?"

"I did not tell you where she was going. Nor do I intend to do so."

Connor began a threatening: "Look here, Professor, this won't do, you know. I guess you don't realise what you're saying."

"I do," the little man broke in, with simple dignity, "and I am prepared to take the consequences."

"You're letting yourself in for something pretty unpleasant," Connor snorted, "as an accessory after the crime. Why should you want to shield this girl? She's nothing to you."

"I allowed the girl to escape because I felt – for several reasons – that it was the wisest course for all parties," the professor answered. "As you know, Mr Connor, the locals are in an exceedingly excited condition at present, owing to certain irrigation schemes."

Connor and Bustard glanced at each other and nodded. "The Pueblo views these irrigation schemes with hatred and suspicion," the professor's dry voice went on meaningly. "If you will reflect for a moment, I fancy you will agree with me that to bring a Pueblo

Indian to trial for murder at this crucial time would be more than unwise. It would be dangerous."

"That's so," Bustard put in. "There's a lot in what he says, Mr Connor."

Connor rubbed his chin thoughtfully. "It will be mighty hard to catch her now," he agreed. "But I guess we better send out a posse. You see, there's the pearls..." He broke off as Stephen Pine banged his fist on the table, sending pens and pencils rattling to the floor, and sprang to his feet.

"Damn the pearls!" Steve roared, purple in the face. "What the hell do I care for the pearls! My wife has been murdered and you sit here wasting time, discussing whether or not you'd better arrest the murderess. If you don't get after that damn girl pretty quick I'll attend to her myself. I'll smoke out every pueblo between here and Panama, and hang that girl to the highest tree in Tecos if it takes every cent I have in the world!"

"Mr Pine," Professor Bridges broke in, so solemnly that Stephen paused in spite of himself. "Mr Pine, your anger is only natural and does you credit. But before you urge these extreme measures I would have you recall one or two recent trials for murder that have made the United States the laughing-stock of the world. Do you wish to spend the next six months in New Mexico while a *cause célèbre* drags its slimy length through one court after another? Do you wish to have your past life scrutinized under the microscope of the counsel for the defence? Will Mr Atwater enjoy being questioned by unscrupulous lawyers intent on creating an unfavourable impression of the family for the benefit of the jury?"

Algy stirred uneasily. "There's something in what he says, Uncle Steve," he put in, with a glance at Mr Carboy that brought a nod of agreement.

But Steve flung up his head, straightening his shoulders, his jaws came together with a snap and he spoke through clenched teeth: "I don't give a damn for what happens to you, Algy. As for me – I'll have to face the music, and to hell with the consequences!

If they find out I've been a swine – well, it can't be helped."

"Mr Pine," the professor remarked, "you forget another person who will share in the horrors of this murder trial. As one of Mrs Kearny-Pine's heirs, even Miss Colbrook cannot hope to escape suspicion. She will be subjected to the vilest insinuations."

"That is true," Carboy remarked. "Only too true."

"Rosalie?" Steve muttered uncertainly, and turned to Pierce. "What do you say, Hubert? Do I have to take this awful thing sitting down, because of Rosalie? Let poor Louisa's murderess go scot free without lifting a finger?"

"Well, Steve," Pierce said slowly, "in a present day murder trial the innocent often suffer with the guilty. It would be a terrible experience for Rosalie..."

"Gentlemen," the district attorney broke in stiffly. "The matter is in my hands and I propose to do my duty without consulting any one of you. I shall send a posse after this girl Bella, and if she is apprehended I promise to stage a trial that will surprise your effete Easterners. A trial with none of the prolonged sliminess which Professor Bridges anticipates. The West does not copy New York and New Jersey in legal matters... And now, Mr Pine, you and Mr Atwater are excused, you will wish to make arrangements for your departure tomorrow. You are at liberty to leave Tecos – with the understanding that you will return if necessary. You may tell Miss Colbrook that the murder, thanks to Professor Bridges, is no longer a mystery. It will be a relief to her mind."

Stephen Pine rose reluctantly. He stood, hesitating for a moment, as if about to speak. Then he thought better of it, turned on his heel and went heavily out of the room, followed by Algy Atwater.

The district attorney waited until they had gone, and then turned to Bustard. "Bustard," he said sharply, "go out in the hall and see if James Rio is still there. If he is, bring him in – and step lively!"

Bustard departed, and returned at once with James Rio, who

planted himself stolidly in front of the table. Connor gave him a long scrutinizing look but his face was empty of expression.

"James Rio," Connor said. "A lady was murdered here in the hotel a few days ago."

"Yes. I have heard that a lady was murdered in the hotel."

"Did you know her? Had she visited the Pueblo?"

"She came to the Pueblo one day, and I acted as guide. She gave me two dollars when she went away."

"James Rio, did you know that this lady was killed by one of your people?" The question was snapped out like a whiplash, but it brought only a puzzled stare. As Connor went on, "She was killed by Bella, the girl who works here in the hotel," bewilderment gave way to such utter amazement that Pierce, watching closely, was convinced James Rio's surprise was genuine.

"Bella?" James Rio said slowly, "Bella? But why? Why should Bella wish to kill the lady? What harm had the lady done to Bella? Who says that Bella killed the lady?"

"Professor Bridges says so."

James Rio's dark eyes, expressionless now, moved slowly to the professor's face and back again to Connor's, as the latter went on: "It's a long story and I haven't time for all of it now. The gist of it is this, Professor Bridges met Bella hiding on the Mountain this morning, and she confessed to him that she had killed the lady because Wind-from-the-Mountain told her to."

"Wind-from-the-Mountain? But Wind-from-the-Mountain is dead!"

"We know that," Connor said impatiently. "We also know that Wind-from-the-Mountain discovered – or thought he had discovered – that this lady here at the hotel was the daughter of General Kearny, the general who ordered the execution of Desert Eagle. All his life – as I guess you know without me telling you – Wind-from-the-Mountain had nursed his hate and hoped for revenge. At last he got it. Through Bella. And died of joy when she brought him the news."

"But the girl Bella..." James Rio began eagerly. And broke off. He stood silent for a moment, his eyes on the ground. Then he looked up, his broad face expressionless, raised a solemn hand, let it drop.

"It is well," he said, and his words fell heavily, weighted with resignation. "It is well. A good end for a great chief. Wind-from-the-Mountain, my grandfather, was a great chief. His way of dying was a good way."

"I'm glad you're satisfied," Connor remarked grimly. "But, as it happens, it is not the death of Wind-from-the-Mountain but the murder of Mrs Kearny-Pine that I want to talk about."

"You mean?" James Rio's voice was anxious now.

"You know damn well what I mean. Murder is murder, no matter what the cause may be. This lady was killed by one of your people and the Pueblo will be held responsible. You've got to help me all you know how."

"But what can I do, Mr Connor? Wind-from-the-Mountain is dead and buried. You would not wish me to dig him up again?"

Connor shook his head. "The great chief can rest in peace for all of me," he grinned. "It's the girl I'm after."

"Bella? Then you have not caught her? Bella is a bad girl. I will go to the Pueblo and bring her back to you. She is a bad girl. She has brought shame to her people." He turned as if to leave the room, but Connor stopped him.

"That's damn nonsense, James Rio. You know as well as I do that the girl wouldn't be such a fool as to hang around the Pueblo after committing murder."

"Then she is still hiding on the Mountain. I will find her in two-three hours. She has no horse. She cannot go far without a horse."

"Well, as a matter of fact, Connor admitted, "we have reason to think she managed to get hold of a horse. When last seen, she was making for one of the big pueblos to the south."

"Then it will not be so easy. If the girl gets to Laguna or Acoma, it will be like looking for one leaf in the autumn woods."

"That's right. But we got to do our best. I'm sending out a posse and…"

"I will go with you. My horse is fast. I will…"

"No. I don't want you to go yourself," Connor said, and James Rio's face fell. "You can pick out a couple of your smartest men and I'll take 'em along as guides. But you're needed right here on the spot. I want you to get back to the Pueblo quick's ever you can, and keep things quiet. I bet you have a hell of a time doing it! But I don't need to remind you…" Connor paused and threw Bustard a significant glance over his shoulder, answered by the latter with an emphatic nod. "You know mighty well, James Rio, with that irrigation scheme the way it is, this is no time for a row."

"I understand, Mr Connor."

"When the news of what's happened gets about, there's liable to be bad feeling in Tecos – Mr Bustard will take care of that and see that it don't lead to any trouble. But I'm depending on you to put the lid on the Pueblo. Tell 'em whatever you've a mind to – lies or the truth. Anything, so long's you keep the pot from boiling over. See? Now clear out. I got a lot to do."

James Rio nodded gravely, bowed right and left, and moved towards the door. As he reached it, he paused and turned.

"Love. Money. Revenge," he said solemnly. "Three good reasons for killing. But revenge is the best."

Pierce watched him go with a puzzled frown.

19

Stephen was so unspeakably thankful to be getting away from Tecos at last that he overflowed with good will and offered accommodations in his private car waiting at Lamy to any travellers who wanted to return to the East. Most of them, including the various Golden Chain magnates and their followers, accepted with gratitude. But Hubert Pierce and Mr Carboy declined. This happened to be a first Western trip for both and they thought, as long as they were here, they might as well have a look around. Professor Bridges, to whom Steve was, of course, peculiarly grateful, had been tempted by the offer of a compartment but finally decided against it. He was anxious to meet a botanist in Santa Fe who had pooh-poohed the possibility of a new species of *Serapias* with such arrogance that the professor couldn't resist putting him in his place. Nor was Mr Wurtz one of Steve's party. Steve had forgotten to invite him – as usual, the little parson had been completely overlooked.

But even with these defections, the party that assembled in the hall immediately after an early breakfast was large and imposing. Four cars were waiting in front of the hotel. Pedro and Lost Arrow ran about, whispering and laughing – tips were coming thick and fast, as they hurried up and down the stairs, bringing Rosalie's tennis rackets, her bags of scarlet and green leather; Miss Gryce's neat suitcase; all the tea baskets, dressing cases and hat boxes, relics of poor Mrs Kearny-Pine, whose comfort in travelling had demanded a separate receptacle for almost every article she possessed; Steve's bags and fishing rods; the impedimenta of the magnates and their staff, and the easel, colour box, umbrella and canvases belonging to John Greenough.

For John Greenough was, of course, going East with Rosalie.

He knew that his big pictures of the Rancho and Canyon del Oro would never be finished now, for Rosalie's memories of Tecos would make return impossible. But what did that matter? Art was no longer important. Put Rosalie in one scale and art in the other, and art would go up like a balloon. He could think of nothing but Rosalie and was intent only on making these moments of departure as easy for her as possible.

Miss Gryce had also decided to return to New York, though very very unwillingly. She felt pretty low in her mind as she stood waiting in the hall. But she knew that she had escaped arrest by a narrow margin. Pierce had told her that the telegram from the 'Infant Paupers' had actually been in his hand, ready for the district attorney, when Professor Bridges appeared on the scene as opportunely as Isaac's guardian angel and substituted the real criminal for herself. Mr Pierce had warned her that this didn't mean she was out of the woods. Not by any means. He would do his best for her, but only on one condition. She must face the music; return to New York, confess and make restitution. There was no way out. She had consented.

Algy Atwater, on the other hand, was more than willing to leave Tecos. He had given up his studio and planned to spend a few months in New York while he decided just which portion of the globe would provide the most piquant stimulus to his art. For Algy did not – he told Miss Joy and Mr Magilp – expect to abandon art altogether. Probably he would not be able to give art his undivided attention as in the past. A man with money had so many demands on his time, but he would always have a studio. Perhaps in Madagascar. Perhaps in Venice. And there was a lot to be said for Bali and the Fiji Islands. Anyway, Algy said he was fed up with Tecos as he invited Miss Joy and Mr Magilp to pay him a visit in Madagascar, Venice, Bali or the Fiji Islands.

For in spite of the early hour, Miss Joy and Mr Magilp and all the other artists had come to bid goodbye to Rosalie and John Greenough. The hall was crowded. Mrs Couch was there waiting to speed the parting guests – and waiting impatiently enough. She longed to see the last of Stephen Pine and his family and begin a drastic house cleaning that would dissipate any scent of crime that might still taint the atmosphere, write new advertisements that would refill the hotel in double quick time, and do a lot of other things that would bring good out of evil. For Mrs Couch was hopeful as well as impatient: in a million homes from the Atlantic to the Pacific the Blue Santo Hotel was now as well known as Plymouth Rock or Radio City. She told herself that the cloud darkening her business for the past week was lined with solid silver; it might even burst into Danae's shower of gold.

It seemed as if the party would never get off. But at length Pedro announced that the motors were packed and ready. Everybody shook hands with everybody else all over again. The travellers, emerging, found several reporters and cameras facing them on the sidewalk. For although the solution of the murder mystery was being read at many breakfast tables, the story could be indefinitely continued. It would be a long long time before Rosalie could pick up a Sunday newspaper without finding her own face staring back at her, nor could she expect to win a tennis tournament or appear at a horse show without being described as "the beautiful Miss Colbrook, whose aunt Mrs Kearny-Pine," etc, etc.

The cars moved away from the door, followed by suppressed cheers, for all the small boys of Tecos and most of the inhabitants were gathered in the square to witness the departure of the family who had provided such a thrilling interlude in monotonous lives. Old as well as young would have given vent to their gratitude if they had not been restrained by propriety, remembering that the family were in mourning.

As the car turned into the highroad Rosalie Colbrook looked back. Between tall cottonwoods the Pueblo showed for a moment, golden in the sunlight against the somber blue of Tecos Mountain, and was gone. She relaxed with a sigh of relief.

In the meantime another group of travellers – those who

planned to take the usual train from Lamy after spending the day in Santa Fe – were gathering in the hall. Pedro and Lost Arrow had assembled their luggage and now began packing the car that had drawn up outside as soon as the Pine automobiles drove away. But no curious crowd on the sidewalk watched the process, and for the first time in several days, the hotel, inside and out, was free from reporters. They too had melted away with the departure of the principals in the tragedy. Hubert Pierce had come downstairs and was having a last word with the district attorney and the sheriff, who were staying in Tecos until later in the day. Miller peered out from behind the desk. Mrs Couch and Professor Bridges, vasculum and plant-press at his feet, stood chatting at a front window while he kept close watch on Pedro's handling of his other packages of botanical treasures.

Pedro finished the job and was re-entering the hall when another departing guest, the Reverend Mr Wurtz, came downstairs carrying his bag; Pedro took it from him. Professor Bridges picked up his vasculum and plant-press and moved to the door. But, to his obvious surprise, found himself in collision with Bustard, who had planted himself in the way.

"I beg your pardon," the professor murmured, trying to pass, but Bustard laid a hand on his shoulder and let out a singsong chant:

"Thomas Bridges," he droned, "I arrest you for the murder of Louisa Kearny-Pine and warn you that anything you say may be used against you."

Mrs Couch screamed. The professor placed his vasculum and plant-press on a table and turned to the district attorney.

"And what, Mr Connor, is the meaning of this farce, this outrage?" he demanded.

Connor waved his hand. "Don't ask me," he said blandly. "I'm not responsible. Ask Mr Pierce."

The professor fixed his reproving gaze on Pierce's face. "Mr Pierce, I am amazed," he said sadly. "Simply amazed. This is unworthy of you. Realizing, I presume, that the arrest of a poor

Indian girl would bring you but little kudos, you have selected a more prominent victim. But why, groping in the dark, did you hit on me? Why not Miss Spingle, or Miss Burleigh, or Mr Clark?"

"Because," Pierce answered, "since last evening I have not been groping in the dark. Till then, I confess, the light was dim. I got a glimmer when I studied the various hotel guests. You were the only clever one of the lot. You were a rich professor – orchid raising is an expensive hobby, and professors are seldom rich. Had you been speculating? I learned that you were well known in Wall Street and had lost heavily in the Peerless crash. Just what did that imply? The closing of your orchid house, the end of your scientific experiments, the work of a lifetime come to nothing. So I could give you one motive – pressing need for money! Who was responsible for your ruin? Mrs Kearny-Pine, owner of the Golden Chain. I could give you another motive – revenge!"

Pierce paused expectantly. But the professor's sad calm remained unbroken, and Pierce went on: "You are not impressed, I see. No doubt you are saying to yourself that this is all theory. Very well then, let us leave theory and proceed to fact."

Pierce moved to the table, glanced at the vasculum and turned to the professor with a grim smile.

"It interests me," he said, "to note that your tin case is green, Professor. I have been hoping to discover 'something green' which would connect you with two other crimes – we must have a little talk re painting stools and liqueur bottles. But that can wait. At the moment I have more important fish to fry – or, rather to find – and a vasculum seems an unlikely hiding place for the sort of specimen I'm looking for. It's too damp. Now this," he went on, "would do very nicely," and he picked up the plant-press.

"Leave that alone!" the professor snarled. "Dried plants are extremely fragile. Careless handling would work irreparable damage!"

But Pierce ignored the protest. He loosened the straps that held the slatted boards together, turned the press upside down and let the contents – sheets of grey blotting paper, bunches of dried flowers and leaves – flutter out. From among them something shimmering and milk white slid snakelike to the floor.

Pierce stooped, rose, and held out his hand. "The pearls," he said. "I hoped that you would feel so safe you'd try to make a getaway!"

"I have no idea how they came there," the professor said. "They must have been planted. For all I know they were planted by the police."

Pierce shook his head, thrust thumb and finger into his breast pocket, drew out a small glittering object and held it out for all to see. "The clasp," he said. "You forget, my dear sir, that you yourself presented us with the clasp of the necklace!"

The professor bit his lip, but instantly recovered himself and stood with folded arms, his eyes on the floor, as Pierce handed over the pearls and the clasp to the district attorney.

Connor took them with a grunt of satisfaction. "So you guessed right, Mr Pierce," he said admiringly. "I must say, I had my doubts when you suggested this trap. But you certainly guessed right. I congratulate you."

"Yes, I guessed right," Pierce smiled. Then taking pity on Mrs Couch, who seemed on the point of exploding with questions, he turned to her. "How did I guess?" he said. "Well, for one thing, I didn't believe Bella was guilty. She did not fit into my theory that the murder of Mrs Kearny-Pine was connected with the killing of Marie the maid. Bella could not have killed Marie, she never remains in the hotel at night."

"Marie!" Mrs Couch exclaimed. "Was Marie murdered?"

"It amounts to that. She was doped so that the necklace could be stolen. But I'll tell you about that later. To return to Bella, another thing that made me sure of her innocence was James Rio's expression last evening when he was told she was guilty. Just for a second he let the mask slip; I caught a flash of contemptuous incredulity – instantly wiped out – it was safer to agree with whatever Mr

Connor said. But I might have missed that flash if I hadn't been on the lookout for it. You see, I happened to know that the professor's story was a tissue of lies from beginning to end."

Pierce turned to the professor. "Your tale was clever, Bridges," he went on. "But it had one fatal flaw. If you had known what I knew you would never have invented your yarn of sacred images and revengeful Indians – nor, as a matter of fact, would Mr Connor and Mr Bustard have believed it, if they had known what I knew. I knew that the image of the Blue Santo, the very keystone of your edifice, was not a genuine antique, for Mrs Couch had told me."

"So I did!" Mrs Couch cried. "And I never put two and two together. How could I have been so dumb!"

"Of course," Pierce went on, "if the image was a modern fake it could not have belonged to General Kearny, nor would it be considered sacred by anybody. But there is still one point that I should like cleared up, Professor, just why did you decide to provide us with a red herring and lead us off the track?" He paused encouragingly, but meeting only a stare that Medusa would have envied, smiled, "Ah well, I dare say you are wise to let no crumb of information escape you," and stopped as if he had nothing more to say.

But Mrs Couch was not satisfied. "Why did he make up that story about poor Bella?" she asked.

"He got a shock when he returned to his room the evening of the inquest and saw it had been searched for the second time. I had gone through all the hotel rooms, of course, after Mrs Kearny-Pine's body was found and, everywhere, I took care to leave traces of my visits; faint traces that would pass unnoticed by the innocent, but that a guilty person would spot at once and find so alarming he would be spurred to action. The trick worked. As for his story, it was undoubtedly suggested by Bella's most opportune elopement. Yes, she really did elope with her lover. He learned that fact, somehow or other, and made use of it."

"Bella's family must have known of the elopement."

"Of course they did. James Rio never believed the story for a moment, but he decided it would be safer not to meddle, let the authorities find out about Bella for themselves."

Pierce turned to the district attorney. "That is all I have to say for the present, Mr Connor. The prisoner may be removed."

WANT TO READ MORE CLASSIC DETECTIVE FICTION FROM THE GOLDEN AGE OF CRIME?

WWW.LOSTCRIMECLASSICS.COM
FEATURES A FANTASTIC COLLECTION OF REDISCOVERED CRIME NOVELS.

IF YOU ENJOYED THIS BOOK YOU MIGHT ALSO LIKE:

READ ON FOR THE EXCITING FIRST CHAPTER OF

THE MAN WITH NO FACE

ALL BOOKS AVAILABLE THROUGH WWW.LOSTCRIMECLASSICS.COM OR FROM AMAZON.

1

"Lady Isabel put it to her cheek,
Sae did she to her chin;
Sae did she to her rosy lips,
And the rank poison gaed in."

SCOTTISH BALLAD

Mr Minton Marbury finished his second cup of coffee and laid down his napkin with a sense of satisfaction and anticipation. Breakfast could not have been better. An interesting morning lay before him. Sunshine had come at last after a week of rain, bringing a typical New York March day of glittering distances and high white clouds hurrying across a blue sky. Mr Marbury glanced out of the dining-room window, observed that another crocus had come up during the night, and gave himself to blissful contemplation of the back yard.

For the back yard, after months of care and more expense than Mr Marbury wished to remember, was no longer a back yard. It was a garden. Where, for some thirty years – half his life in fact – he would have seen a space of grey flagstones criss crossed by clotheslines, smelling of cats, dusty and yet mysteriously damp, he now saw an agreeable arrangement of grass plots, flower beds, shrubs, sundial and slim dark cedar trees. The grass was already green, the flower beds prickled with green sprouts, the shrubs hinted of pink and white glory to come.

No wonder Mr Marbury smiled! He was about to sally forth to count his crocuses when a maid came in with a message. Mrs Beaumont had phoned to say she'd got the letter from Scotland and she was expecting Mr Marbury to tea.

He nodded and subsided into his chair again. This message from Clare Beaumont meant a change of the day's plans. He had intended to spend the morning in the garden and devote the afternoon to examination of the stamps and coins that were to be sold at the Busby auction tomorrow. However, it would never do to disappoint Clare. The letter from Scotland would revive her interest in genealogy, and she would want her coats of arms at once. Dear Clare was so impatient! There was a morning's work on them. He must start painting as soon as he had read his *Times*. The garden would have to wait.

So eleven o'clock found Mr Marbury in the library. His long thin back and sleek head were bent over his painting table, pince-nez tight clenched to his long thin nose, long thin hand delicately manipulating a watercolour brush as he added dashes of azure, blobs of gules and specks of sable to the various crests, helmets, wreaths and mantles that ornamented the coat of armour of Clare Beaumont's ancestors. Mr Marbury was enjoying himself. He liked illuminating, he liked working for Clare. Clare was a dear. Indeed, more than once since her husband's death five years ago, he had been on the point of proposing but, somehow, he never had.

The morning passed happily away. After an excellent lunch, and a brief siesta, Mr Marbury adjusted his top hat to an exact angle and stepped out into the sun and wind of East Sixty second Street. Clare Beaumont's house was only a few blocks away, farther north and on Fifth Avenue. At five minutes of five he was ringing her doorbell. As the empire clock on the mantelpiece chimed the hour he was seated in her library, waiting – as he had so often waited – for dear Clare. She was far too apt to ignore the passing of time.

Not that Mr Marbury minded waiting. After a busy morning, it was pleasant to relax in a deep armchair and in such agreeable surroundings. Clare's taste was perfect. There wasn't another room in New York, he reflected, that so exquisitely combined elegance and comfort. The somber beauty of books lined three walls, tall windows gave glimpses of the park's treetops, from a panel over the fireplace a magnificent Raeburn – Clare's great-great grandfather, Robert Bell of Irongray, in red coat and riding breeches – beamed down, mellow as his own port. An aromatic whiff of southern fat wood came from the fire sparkling on the hearth and mingled with the scent from vases of roses and mignonette and a row of potted plants on the window sills. A perfect setting for Clare, he thought. Like Clare, beautiful and yet comfortable.

The door opened and Mr Marbury sat erect. But it was only a footman carrying a tea tray. Mr Marbury watched the arrangement of the tea table with interest. As usual, envying Clare that Paul Revere teapot. Did the covered dish contain cinnamon toast or muffins? Those little pink cakes with citron on the top looked delicious. He was glancing hungrily at the clock when the door opened again, and this time it was Clare herself, smiling as only Clare could smile, soft and glowing and full of life.

They had tea. Clare had never looked lovelier, Mr Marbury said to himself, as she handed him his cup. A soft pink rose such a relief in this age of bones and lipstick. He helped himself to a frosted cake, it was as good as it looked and sat sipping and munching.

"What is that? Saccharine?" he asked in surprise, as she uncorked a small bottle and dropped a pellet into her tea. "Aren't you allowed sugar? I was just thinking how well you looked."

"I am well," she laughed. "Fit as a fiddle. But I'm going to a new man, Doctor Costello, and he has cut out sugar. But don't let's waste time on doctors. Have another cup? No? Then ring the bell for William, please." The tea things were taken away, the table cleared, various portfolios fetched from cupboard drawers and Mr Marbury produced a large envelope from his pocket. One by one the illuminations were displayed, admired and exclaimed over.

"Oh, Minton!" she sighed. "They're too too exquisite! You're simply wonderful! I don't know which I like best. The lrving holly sprigs or that enchanting Cawdor deer, or those sweet sweet lambs and cows and leaves of the Durhams and the mottoes – too fascinating! 'Furth Fortune and Fill the Fetters.' Now isn't that quaint! I can hardly wait to paste them in my book."

Her enthusiasm was most gratifying. Mr Marbury slipped the squares of tinted cardboard back into their envelope with a murmur of satisfaction, feeling amply repaid for his hours of labour.

"Now for the documents," she said. "The letter from the Lord Lyon in Edinburgh and the chart!"

She opened a small white velvet bag that lay in her lap and handed him a letter. He read it. "Very satisfactory," he nodded. "The Heralds' office is always most obliging," and bent over another paper she was unfolding before him on the table.

"Look at this!" she cried triumphantly. "My grandmother was right. This chart says that James Bell was one of the Bells of Irongray, and he came to this country in 1812."

"Robert Bell of Irongray," he read aloud, "born 1765. We know all about that Robert, his son Robert married Ellen Dunbar. Nothing new there... Ah, now we come to something the four children of Robert: James, Andrew, John and Alexander."

"And that James was my great-grandfather," Clare broke in triumphantly. "He came to America and his daughter married Alan Carlisle and their son Alan was my father. The Lord Lyon says so I have a right to the Bell of Irongray arms after all!"

"You certainly have. I'll paint it for you at once."

"You're an angel, Minton, is it a pretty one?"

"Three bells argent on a field azure."

"Blue and silver... very pretty. You know, Minton, it's a real satisfaction to find that my grandmother was right. She was a dear old lady. I remember her perfectly though I was only five when she died... She wore a lace cap and a pearl brooch and she used to sing me Scotch songs. The one I liked best began:

> " 'Bessie Bell and Mary Gray,
> They were twa bonnie lasses.

> *They built a hut upon the brae*
> *And covered it with rashes.'*

"I named my doll 'Mary Gray' and I used to sit under a lilac bush in the garden and make believe we were the lasses in their hut. Dear me, that was more than thirty years ago!"

"You must have been a very pretty child, Clare."

"And I haven't changed much? Minton, you're a darling!"

He smiled. She rattled on. "Isn't it exciting to think the *Record of my Ancestry* is almost done! As soon as I get the dates Mr Angus Bell of Dumfries is looking up for me, I can have it bound in green morocco, I think, with a little gold tooling. Could you help me get the pages in proper order, Minton? What about tomorrow?"

But before he could answer, there was a knock at the door and William the footman came in.

"Mr Wheeler is on the phone, madam," he said. "He has a lease for you to sign and he hopes tomorrow afternoon about five will be convenient."

"It won't be," Mrs Beaumont frowned. "But I suppose I shall have to see him. Tell him he can come, William."

"Mr Wheeler? Atwood's clerk?" Marbury asked.

"Yes. Mr Atwood told me there would be some papers to sign and I must be sure to read every one of them all through. That means Mr Wheeler will be here for ages, and my book must wait for a day or two. Tomorrow I'm sitting for my portrait. Jim Northcote gave me no peace until I let him paint me. And the next day, oh, well, I'll have to call you up. By the way, there's something I want to consult you about. I am..."

Again the footman appeared. "Mr Northcote," he said, let in a tall good looking young man, and departed. "We were just speaking of you, Jim," Mrs Beaumont exclaimed. "This is Mr Marbury, a very old friend of mine."

"How's the portrait getting on?" Marbury asked as they shook hands.

"We've made a very good beginning, I think," Northcote answered. "Mrs Beaumont seems to like it."

"It's simply wonderful!" she cried. "Not too *modern* and yet not one bit *vieux jeu*. Just the happy medium between Bouguereau and Gauguin. You must come and see it, Minton."

"I'll be delighted." Marbury rose. "Good-bye, Clare. You'll call me up?"

"As soon as I have a free afternoon. Good-bye, and thank you a thousand times for the illuminations."

Handsome fellow, that young Northcote, Marbury said to himself as he left the room. Nice blue eyes. I like him. Hope I'll see him again.

Next morning, true to his word, Mr Marbury finished illuminating the Bell of Irongray arms. But Clare Beaumont did not ring him up that evening. She seemed to have forgotten him. Two days went by. Three. And still she did not telephone. On the fourth day he rang up her house. There was a long wait. Then came a voice – a high, breathless, horrified voice – William's voice?

"Hello! Hello! Yes. Mrs Beaumont's house... No. No. She can't come... Oh, is that you, Mr Marbury? Something awful has happened here, sir! Awful! Awful! The police..."

Sudden silence. Marbury rang again and again. There was no answer. He hung up the receiver with a shaking hand.

"Good God!" he muttered. "William was evidently in a terrible state. Something's wrong. What can it be? The police are there. A burglary, I suppose. I'd better go around."

Ten minutes later he was standing on Mrs Beaumont's steps waiting for an answer to his ring. There was a brief delay and when at length the door opened he was confronted by a policeman.

"Nobody allowed in," the man said.

"But what has happened, officer? I'm an intimate friend of Mrs Beaumont's. I might be of some assistance. Will you just tell her I'm here?"

The man hesitated. Then: "It'll be in the evening papers," he said. "So there's no harm my telling you. Mrs Beaumont is dead, sir."

Marbury turned white, and caught at the railing.

"When?" he gulped.

"Between nine and ten this morning. Committed suicide."

"No! No!" Mr Marbury shuddered. "Impossible. There must be some mistake."

The policeman shook his head. "It's a fact, sir. The doctors are here now, and the lawyer. And no one else is to be let in."

Mr Marbury turned and walked stiffly away. As he crossed the street a taxi driver shouted at him, but Marbury did not see the man's angry face as it whizzed past perilously close. He was back again in Clare Beaumont's library four days ago, he felt her soft hand in his as she bade him good-bye, heard her laughing voice: "Thank you a thousand times, Minton. You're an angel." Clare dead? No! No!

He had almost reached his own house when he remembered that the policeman had said, "It will all be in the evening paper." There was a newsboy at the corner. He retraced his steps and bought a couple of papers. But he did not dare to glance at them. Folding them under his arm, he walked toward home, head bent.

"I beg your pardon!"

He looked up. He had collided with a man. Someone he knew, Northcote, Jim Northcote.

Northcote held an open newspaper in his hand. The two stood staring at each other. Then:

"I see you've heard," Northcote muttered.

Marbury nodded. "Only the – the fact. I haven't looked at the papers. What do they say?"

"That it was suicide!" Northcote exclaimed. "A damn newspaper lie, of course. It's incredible. Why, I saw her yesterday and she was as gay as a lark. I simply don't believe it."

"I agree. There must be some mistake. But I've just been to her house... Couldn't get in... The doctor was there..."

"Damn the doctor! If all the doctors in New York swore it was suicide till they were black in the face, I wouldn't believe it. As for these vile reporters..." Northcote crumpled the newspaper angrily into a ball. "I'd like to thrash every man jack of them."

"This is my house," Marbury said. "Come in, won't you? I'd like to talk it over."

Neither spoke again until they were in the library. Marbury indicated a chair in silence. They sat down. Then he resolutely unfolded his newspaper. Flaring headlines ran across the front page:

"Suicide on Fifth Avenue. Mrs Arthur Beaumont. Prominent in Society. Widow of Wall Street Magnate. Colony Club. Piping Rock." And so on and so on, for a dozen lines. Then, at last, the story, brief enough in all conscience:

"The body was found at half past nine this morning by Miss Jane Grant, Mrs Beaumont's personal maid, when she entered the bedroom in order to remove the breakfast tray she had taken in at nine, Mrs Beaumont having, as usual, breakfasted in bed. Dr Carter of 183 Park Avenue was summoned at once and arrived within a few minutes, but could be of no assistance as Mrs Beaumont was already dead. Poison, probably cyanide of potassium, self administered, is believed to be the cause of death. A note found on the dressing table stated that the unfortunate lady had decided to commit suicide. No arrangements have as yet been made for the funeral."

Mr Marbury read the paragraph thrice over, then looked up to meet Jim Northcote's inquiring gaze.

"Well, what do you think of it?" Northcote asked.

"I don't seem able to think," Mr Marbury quavered. "Here it is in black and white, and yet I can't believe it. I can't take it in. Clare commit suicide? It's incredible!"

"You've said it," Northcote nodded. "It's incredible."

"But it seems she left a letter saying she intended to kill herself."

"So they say. But do you notice how brief the account is? I bet they're hushing things up. There's material for a column and only the bare facts are given."

"That is true."

"They don't tell us whether Mrs Beaumont seemed as usual when the maid brought her breakfast. Or suggest any reason for believing it to be suicide – except the note. They don't give the contents of the note, or say whether it was in her handwriting."

"That is implied."

"Well, do you know of any reason? Was Mrs Beaumont in any financial difficulties? Or mixed up with shady people who might blackmail her? Might she have become involved in an unhappy love affair?"

"Good God, no! Atwood, her lawyer, told me a few days ago that she was the only one of his clients who had not suffered from the depression. As for the other reasons, good God, no!"

"Which brings us back to our original proposition; the suicide theory is untenable. Well, we shall know more after the inquest."

"I suppose there will have to be an inquest?"

"Undoubtedly. And I advise you to attend, Mr Marbury. I most certainly shall. Look here, if the inquest doesn't clear things up – and I have a feeling it won't – may I come and talk it all over with you?"

"Of course, of course."

"Thanks. Good-bye," and Northcote was gone.

Mr Marbury went to the window. Northcote was already in the street, striding along at a great rate. "What energy," Marbury murmured. "Did I ever walk as fast as that, I wonder? Good Lord, how old I feel today," and he returned wearily to his armchair.

"Well, I was right," Jim Northcote said. The inquest was over. He had joined Marbury in the street and they were walking along together. "We don't know any more than we did before. That inquest was a farce. No desire whatever to get at the truth. Looked to me as if the lawyers and doctors just wanted to finish the thing up and get home to lunch. I still feel sure that it was not suicide."

"The letter didn't convince you?"

"No. It may have been forged."

"Mr Atwood and Doctor Costello and Jane Grant all identified the handwriting."

"They aren't experts. Anyway, I still maintain that no woman in perfect health of mind and body, of an unusually sunny disposition and with everything to live for, could by any possibility have killed herself. Another point, how would she have got hold of that poison, cyanide, or whatever it was?"

Marbury sighed. "I can explain that," he admitted. "At one time Clare Beaumont was interested in photography. I used to help her develop the negatives. There might have been some cyanide in her dark room."

Northcote shook his head gloomily. They walked on for another block in silence. Then Marbury said: "It might have been an accident."

"Cyanide of potassium get into food by accident? Out of the question! Now, you see where all this lands us? If it was neither suicide nor an accident, it was murder. Someone killed her."

"It certainly looks that way." Marbury shuddered.

"Well then, who would benefit by her death? Who gets her money? Several millions, wasn't it?"

"I fancy so. Some of it, I know, goes to a cousin, or rather, a cousin of her husband's. A Mrs Chase of Baltimore who is enormously rich already, as it happens. The rest is left to various charities. I don't know the details."

"A cousin of her husband's? Then she had no immediate family?"

"No. She was singularly alone in the world. An only child. Father and mother dead. No near relations. Hosts of friends and acquaintances, of course."

"Who was the most intimate?"

"Well, I suppose I was. I've known Clare Beaumont for years. We had many tastes in common. Gardening, genealogy." Mr Marbury's voice broke. He cleared his throat, went on, "Mrs Harcourt and Miss Alice Hemmingway were old friends of hers, and General Blanchard was there a good deal, and oh, any number of people! Clare was the soul of hospitality and everyone liked her."

"I see. What about the servants? Seven or eight of them, I suppose?"

"About that. I don't know any of them well except Clare's maid, Jane Grant, and William, the second man. All of them had been with her for years, except Green, the butler. He was new. Her old butler died not long ago. William is his son."

"A very respectable lot, I gather?"

"Oh, quite. I have a great regard for Jane, and for William too. They were both devoted to Clare."

"It would be interesting to know what Jane really thinks," Northcote said meditatively. "Didn't you feel that she might be keeping something back at the inquest?"

Mr Marbury did not answer at once, for they had reached his house. When they were seated in the library, he said: "To go back to what we were saying, I did think that Jane's testimony at the inquest was remarkably brief. I'll try to see her later on and..."

"Not later on," Northcote broke in, "but at the first possible moment, as soon as the police will let you into the house. There's no time to lose."

Mr Marbury stared. "Surely you don't think it's up to me to interfere? After all, I'm not a relation."

"You just said she hadn't any relations." There was a tinge of impatience in Northcote's voice. "No relations and very few intimate friends. No one, in short, who cares a damn whether or not the poor darling killed herself, except you – and me."

Mr Marbury only sighed and twiddled his eye glasses.

Northcote went on:

"And we both feel dissatisfied with the coroner's verdict of suicide. Well then, it seems to me a spot of investigating is in order. Suppose you make some inquiries and I quest around a bit, and we pool the results. Don't you feel it's a duty? A duty to the dead?"

"I-I suppose it is."

"That's settled then. Now let's make some notes." Jim Northcote produced a sheet of paper and a pencil from his pocket. "We'll make a list of the persons who ought to be questioned."

"Questioned?"

"We must get a record of the last few days of Mrs Beaumont's life. Find out where she went, whom she saw, what she did, the letters she received. All persons able to throw light on any of these points must be questioned. Now, who shall we put first?"

"The police?"

"Just so. A: the police. And then comes Mrs Beaumont's lawyer, I suppose, Mr Atwood. What is his address?"

"Samuel Atwood, 143 Wall Street."

"B: S. Atwood," Northcote wrote. "Who's next? The doctors? There were two of them; Carter, the man the servants sent for in a hurry, and her own physician, Doctor Costello: they come under C. And D brings us to the servants, more particularly Jane and William. Who else? Some clergyman, perhaps. I have an idea that Mrs Beaumont went to St. Margaret's."

"She did. Dr Brace, the rector, is an old friend of Clare's."

"Good. Then E is Dr Brace. Anybody else?"

"I can't think of anyone."

"That will do to begin with, anyway. Now, let's make a plan of campaign and divide forces. I know a man on the Times who would help me with the police. I'll see him tonight, get in touch with the police and find out what they found out, or think they found out, and, if possible, get a look at that suicide letter. And I have another friend who is an interne at the Medical Center and

I'll ask him whether those two doctors have good reputations, and then I'll interview them. Who will you see?"

"Suppose I talk to the rector, Dr Brace, and Mr Atwood? I know them both fairly well."

"All right. Try to persuade Mr Atwood to let us see the servants as soon as possible."

"He won't let anyone into the house until after the funeral in all probability. Atwood is a rigid sort of man, and a stickler for professional etiquette."

"We shall have to wait a day or two then. But when Mr Atwood gives permission and you interview the servants, would you mind if I came too?"

"Not a bit. In fact, my dear fellow, if we are to embark on this investigation you will have to supply the impetus. I feel surprisingly weary – Clare's death has been a terrible shock – and, left to myself, I might succumb to inertia."

"Don't worry. You and I make a swell combination, Mr Marbury. I'll provide the brute strength and leave the brain work to you. Between us we're bound to ferret out something. And if we do –" Northcote's face flushed. "If we find that it was not suicide..." He broke off, and sprang to his feet. "May I drop in again tomorrow afternoon? Would two o'clock suit you?"

Mr Marbury hoisted himself out of his armchair. "I'll be here," he said. "By the way, in my interview with Mr Atwood and Dr Brace I suppose I had better not bring up the question of murder?"

"Let's keep our suspicions to ourselves for the present." Northcote turned to the door, and paused. "I was half in love with her, you know," he went on. "She was ten years older than I, but she seemed so young, and she was lovely to look at. Lovely in every way. I was half in love with her."

"So was I," Mr Marbury sighed. "More than half. A great deal more than half."

"Well, good-bye. See you tomorrow."

As the door closed, Mr Marbury remembered that if Jim

Northcote expected to come at two o'clock the next day, he should have been asked to lunch. But not even then, such was the disorder of Mr Marbury's mind, did it occur to him that two o'clock, his time for napping, was a most inconvenient hour for an appointment. He sat staring into the fire, aware that the happiest chapter in his life had come to an end. Murder or suicide, Clare Beaumont was dead.